Baby Face

Heartlines

Heartlines

♥

Ann Ruffell

Baby Face

A Pan Original

First published 1986 by Pan Books Ltd,
Cavaye Place, London SW10 9PG
9 8 7 6 5 4 3 2 1
© Ann Ruffell 1986
ISBN 0 330 29241 2
Printed and bound in Great Britain by
Hunt Barnard Printing, Aylesbury, Bucks

Chapter 1

When you're a different size from everyone else you don't really notice it most of the time. You feel as if you're quite normal. It's only when something happens to show that you're not — like that Saturday when Marie and I went to buy me a skirt – that you realize it.

That sounds as if I'm really peculiar. I'm not. But I don't even make it to five feet tall. Everyone else is about four inches taller, on average, and you'd be surprised the difference it makes. Especially when you try to buy clothes.

'No, Ros,' said Marie definitely. 'You look awful.'

I looked at myself in the mirror of the cubicle. I'd desperately wanted one of those marvellous straight skirts which had little pleats at the back. Okay, so skirts were meant to be long just now, but there was a difference between long and floor level. I looked like something out of the ark. Or probably not even as good as that. Just plain ridiculous.

'And it won't even take up, because of that pleat,' I said.

'At the waist?' said Marie.

I turned the waistband over. How could the same

skirt, which was the right size if you went by hip and waist measurements, look on me as if it had been constructed for someone with mountainous thighs, and on Marie as if it had been moulded to her slim and willowy figure? But I didn't think I looked quite as awful as that skirt suggested. It wasn't, let's face it, made for a four-foot-eleven-inch dwarf.

'I'll just have to make one,' I said. Pity I wasn't better at sewing or I'd feel a bit more enthusiastic at the prospect.

'Yes,' said Marie. However much she's my best friend, she couldn't tell an untruth about the way off-the-peg clothes hang on me. 'I've always liked that green skirt of yours,' she went on. 'Couldn't we find something like that?'

I gave her a withering look. 'Marks and Spencer's *children's* department?' I said.

'Why not?' said Marie. 'Cheaper, too. You do have some advantages, you know.'

I had to laugh. 'What else?'

'You can wear high heels. I can't. I look like the original beanpole in them.'

'Oh, Marie, that's not true. You look marvellous in them. And you're wrong, you know. I can't wear high heels – they hurt!'

'Coward,' said Marie. 'Who cares if they *hurt* if they look good?'

The trouble is that I have size three feet to match my small height, and anything higher than one-inch heels makes me feel as if I'm standing on my toenails, and I can't walk for more than half a mile before my arches drop and I feel as if I'm crippled.

All right, I'm grumbling about something I can't help and ought to make the best of. Like people who moan about straight hair, or having to wear glasses. The difference is you can do something about straight hair, and if you hate glasses you can wear contact lenses.

I've tried vitamins, calcium tablets, herbal remedies, but the sad truth is that if you're too short there's nothing you can do about it.

I've been smaller than everyone else ever since I went to school. The trouble is, just because you *look* younger than everyone else doesn't mean you *feel* younger, and I hated, right from infant school days, being the baby in everyone else's games.

In fact the only advantage I ever remember coming out of this size business was when I was about ten and, hating school, was weeping as I walked there after the Easter holidays.

'Poor little thing,' said one of my classmates, oozing sympathy.

However, they only play up to your small size when it suits them. Another girl in my class – could she have been my worst enemy? – retorted, 'What do you mean, poor little thing? She's ten, the same as us, isn't she?'

I couldn't win.

My mother doesn't have any sympathy either, and you'd think she would because she's only five feet tall herself. How I envy her that extra inch!

'I don't know what you're making all the fuss about,' she'd tell me impatiently. 'Go and do something interesting, stop worrying about clothes and boys and be a bit more assertive. Then no one will walk over you and treat you like a baby.'

'Noticed the difference between my face and yours?' I snarled. It was nasty of me, and I apologized later, but she did understand what I meant. Her hair has gone prematurely grey, which hasn't changed her good looks in the least, but she does look old. Well, mature, I said more tactfully. Whereas my face, with its chubby cheeks, has the babyishness which adds even more unwanted youth to my short size.

Mum laughed. You couldn't really upset her, not about anything like that. She only gets really het up when she hears about any sort of unfairness in the way women are treated. She and Dad have this marvellous arrangement where they share everything – washing, cleaning, ironing, cooking – or rather they tend to share it out between my brothers and me now, which isn't so marvellous.

Brothers!

Something happened to the genes in our family, I always told them fiercely when they started bossing me about, which was unfair to women. They got the extra inches. I got them chopped off. And they're still growing while I, at seventeen, have probably stopped. I can't see myself under any circumstances sprouting another four or five inches before I'm twenty-one, which I think is the age when you stop growing for good.

'You are lucky, having brothers,' said my friend Aileen. 'I've only got two older sisters, and if they bring boyfriends home I have to keep off.'

'At least they're older than you,' I said bitterly. 'I know my brothers look as if they ought to be earning millions on the Stock Exchange or at least on the dole, but Rick is fifteen and Den is only twelve.'

'Twelve!' said Aileen. 'That's not fair. That's too young even for me.'

We laughed, because Aileen is the youngest in our year – by two months. In fact she only scraped into being the right age for it by having her birthday on August 25th.

'*They* look like young men,' I continued, 'but their friends look their proper age, even Rick's. But Den's are the worst. Have you seen a gang of twelve year olds all together? They've all got high-pitched voices, and they hang about like morons. Rick's friends are just the same, only their voices have broken. Just. Even if they did look at me I wouldn't want them to.'

'I,' said Dawn Fraser languidly, 'have three older brothers and their friends don't look at me either.'

'What? They ignore *you*, Dawn?' we all said. Because she looks really dreamy – too dreamy, our teachers say exasperatedly when she puts on that famous sleepy look during lessons which bore her.

However, back to this skirt and my best friend Marie Johnson who is five foot six, willowy, has a near perfect figure and can wear just about anything she fancies straight off the peg.

'By the time I've finished making one it will be out of date,' I gloomed.

9

'I'll make it for you,' offered Marie.

'You wouldn't!'

'I like dressmaking. Skirtmaking. All that sort of thing,' she said.

I wasn't surprised. Marie seems to have an inexhaustible fount of energy, and is good at nearly everything she tries. If she wasn't so nice I'd probably hate her instead of having her for my best friend.

'Well, if you're sure . . .'

'I often make my own. It's cheaper. And I wouldn't offer if I wasn't sure.'

'True. Right, you're on. If we can find material,' I said, even more gloomily, 'knowing my luck.'

'Oh, shut up,' said Marie, amused. 'What's the matter with you today?'

'The same as every day,' I said. 'Only it gets to me some times worse than others. Everyone else is going out with someone. Or even,' I looked at her meaningly, 'some *two*, and I haven't even started on this happy round yet. Do you realize, Marie, that you are the only, absolutely the only, person in the whole world who makes me feel as if I might be seventeen instead of about twelve?'

'My mother *still* makes me feel about twelve,' said Marie.

'And talking of twelve,' I said, to stop myself feeling sorry for myself, 'do you know what Den did yesterday?'

While I was telling her Den's latest awfulness I couldn't help noticing how everyone's head turned when I was with Marie. She's very striking, not just because she's tall but she has this sort of natural style about her, as if she's proud to be alive and proud to be herself.

Perhaps that was what I needed.

I began to hold my head up higher, practised walking round our house like that, which I thought might even be noticeable since Mum's only an inch taller than me.

'Why are you prancing about like that?' said Den suspiciously on Monday evening.

'Oh, for goodness' sake!' I said, bashing him on the hand with his own physics homework.

'Hey! I only meant . . . Mum! She's beating me up again!'

Mum came through from the front room. 'Don't be so silly, Den. How can she possibly beat you up? I do wish you'd stop quarrelling. I like a bit of time to myself when I get home, you know. Have you done the potatoes?'

Sulkily he had to admit he hadn't, and went out to the shed for them, crashing the back door as he went.

'Want a cup of tea, Mum? Hard day?' I said.

'Ooooh!' she groaned, 'don't talk to me about *kids* today. I've just about had enough. And if anyone else says anything clever about teachers having long holidays I shall personally shoot them and dismember them, limb by slow limb.'

'Bad as that?' I sympathized. Mum's very good at teaching and puts her heart and soul into it, so that when people say it's a job which doesn't need any brain, or is done by people who fail at doing anything else, she really goes wild.

'And no, don't you get me any tea. It's Rick's job. I'll

11

shout for him. He's always getting out of things simply because he disappears up to his room and plays those awful records so loudly no one can get through to him.'

'*I'll* nag him. You go and sit down,' I said firmly, leading her back to the settee where she was watching, of all things, *Jackanory* on television. 'Honestly, Mum!'

'I like people reading me stories,' she said, defensively.

'Nobody reads me stories,' I began, then thought, with a wry smile at myself, that if they did I'd probably moan because it would be another proof of people treating me like a baby. I was getting paranoid about this, I thought, hurtling upstairs to hammer on Rick's door. Life was passing me by and if I didn't stop worrying about being too young I'd miss being young before I got old.

Something like that anyway. It's difficult to think with Duran Duran playing at blast-off volume.

'Rick!' I bawled in a microsecond between two thunderous chords.

There weren't many silent microseconds in that particular record so eventually I had to walk in.

He was freaking out with his bass guitar, playing not quite the same notes as the record. It could have been interesting, if you liked atonal music.   ‑

His mouth did some lip-reading practice.

I interpreted it correctly and stalked across the room to turn the volume down. 'Because I've been knocking about half an hour and you still didn't hear and Mum's falling apart with tiredness and you're supposed to get her a cup of tea.'

'Oh, honestly!' said Rick. 'Couldn't you . . . ?'

'You know why,' I said. Frankly, it would have been a whole lot easier to have got the tea myself, but I am in full agreement with Mum's principles and it's almost worth the hassle. Though I think without her blinding example I'd probably relapse into down-trodden, old-fashioned womanhood out of sheer self-defence.

'Oh, *God*!' said Rick, disgusted, and unwrapped the guitar from his neck. He flipped a few switches, leaving the whole apparatus humming and probably ready to explode and blow up the house at any moment, and stomped downstairs without even instructing me to 'get-out-and-don't-touch-anything-leave-my-records-alone', which he usually did.

But Mum caught him as he whirled in with the tea, hoping to dump it and go before she had a chance to make him do anything else. But *Jackanory* was finished, and she grabbed his arm, almost knocking the tea over at the same time.

'Chips and sausages,' she said. 'Now. Den's done the potatoes. Den had better have done the potatoes. We're going out later and I want it early today.'

'I'll go and turn things off,' he said, knowing he was beaten.

'You have five seconds from now,' she said, looking at her watch which had a stop-watch button on the display.

'Honestly, Mum, just a little leeway . . .'

'*Your* leeway would result in no supper for anyone. Four seconds, and that's being generous.'

13

I do agree with Mum and Dad's ideas about work sharing, but there are times when I wish they were a bit more strict about the quality of work achieved. I do like chips and sausages, but twice a week, every week, when it's Rick's and Den's turns to cook, gets a bit monotonous. And Mum's cooking is *really* fantastic. Still, I suppose its comparative rarity makes it the more welcome when it comes.

Me? Oh, well, I try. Only my Spaghetti Bolognese never comes out quite the same as Mum's and the simple French Country Cooking ends up so complicated that I often wish I'd settled for beans on toast instead.

We all have a conference on Sunday, about what we're going to do for the week, and Dad makes a list for the shopping. He's nearer Sainsbury's and the market than Mum and he has a long enough lunch hour. Besides, he enjoys doing it.

So we sit round the table before supper. Not afterwards, because with a stomach full of food you couldn't care less what you get for the rest of the week. Mum and Dad and I sip sherry, Rick gets some if he nags long enough, but Den doesn't unless he can get a swig of Rick's when he's not looking. It's a nice civilized way of preparing a family menu, so long as the person who's on Sunday turn to cook doesn't have too many complicated last minute things to do, in which case he or she will probably growl 'Chips and sausages' when asked what they'd like to do next week, just like Rick or Den.

Then we have to sort out the housework, which might change every week because of people doing other things after school, so it can get quite complicated. Frankly, I switch off at this point, because I find the whole thing totally boring. I just look on our kitchen pin board and find out what's been decided when it's all done. I think Mum does too, and only agrees to all this because it's nice to sit with a sherry at a half-set table. It's Dad who likes all the complicated stuff. You feel that if computers didn't exist he'd have to invent them just so that he could organize his family into a printout.

Perhaps it's a good thing having a computerized Dad, because if you don't mind being organized to a certain extent it does leave you lots of time to do other things. And nobody's all that worried about whether you do your stint when he says you should or at some other time, so long as it gets done on the day it's supposed to. He only does the timetable because he likes organizing it all.

In fact, apart from having brothers – which is a trial I suppose one has to accept – my life is quite happy, apart from the one thing about not having a boyfriend.

So what? Lots of people haven't got boyfriends.

Yes, but at seventeen nobody has *never* had a boyfriend. Not in our form anyway. Except me.

At fourteen, Marie was the first one to go out with someone regularly. But at fourteen nearly everyone else didn't. Nor at fifteen, even. Or perhaps they did at fifteen, because here was Aileen only sixteen since August and going out with someone since before Christmas. Only I think she was just finishing with the someone she'd been going out with since before Christmas. Even the fact that we had had O levels last year didn't seem to put people off during that summer term.

I know there's no such thing as being on the shelf these days, and that people are much more tolerant of people being single and don't call them 'old maids' any more. But I felt I ought to be able to choose to be single, not to have it thrust upon me.

So it wasn't because I didn't want a boyfriend. I would gladly have given up one of my freedoms to do as I like to invest it in someone who cared about me, or just to have someone to go out with. It simply isn't done to go to discos on your own. It was all right when we went in a crowd, or I went with another girl, but now all my friends are partnered and wouldn't want me tagging along behind, gooseberrying and generally lousing things up for them.

It's this baby-faced appearance which puts the boys off.

Once – only once – a bloke in our year actually came over to me and – I presume – started chatting me up. I say I presume, because I only knew from hearsay and this one particular occasion what chatting-up means. About five minutes later, when I had started to glow with pleasure, flattery and confusion, someone called over, very loudly, saying, 'Hey, Vic, pick someone your own size!'

He went, like a stone from one of Den's catapults. If I'd fancied him before, I certainly didn't now, leaving me on the edge of tears but not daring to cry or even get my own friends' sympathy in case they treated me like a baby again.

It tends to make you aggressive, and that puts the boys off.

16

The only ones who are likely to come near me are the little ones. When someone of five-foot nothing comes creeping round, I've only got to look in his eyes to know that he'd really prefer someone like Marie, or Dawn, but since he hasn't got a hope in hell he thinks he might as well try me.

I don't even let them *start* the chatting up bit. I mean, what must we look like together, if I find I feel *tall* next to them? Then my mind goes off in a logical sequence and I start thinking of even more stunted children and all the problems they'd have . . . so let's not let the relationship even begin, so it doesn't have a chance of getting so far that you need to start counting chromosomes.

And in the way life is, the only boys I really fancied at all were so tall that they never even noticed that the little ant somewhere below their towering gaze was me.

Chapter 2

Marie came round that Monday evening with her pattern, so that she could measure me, and it, and make adjustments.

'Wouldn't it be lovely,' I said wistfully, still in a state of depression about my lack of inches, 'if you could make adjustments to *me* and just stitch me up to look right?'

'Stop snivelling,' said Marie, 'and stand still. Listen, Ros, if you wriggle you'll get pins in the back of your knees.'

'Why have I got to have it pinned on me, anyway?' I said, craning my neck round to try and see what she was doing at the back. 'I thought it had lines for you to fold or to let out.'

'It does,' said Marie, 'but I want to make sure it fits *you*.'

'No wonder I never get it right, even when I follow what the pattern says exactly. Sorry,' as I twisted again to see how she did it.

'Keep still or you won't get it done at all. I'm going out with Les in half an hour.'

'Have they met yet?' I asked. Marie had been going out with Les as well as Kevin for the past fortnight. So far she'd managed to keep one from knowing about the other.

'No,' said Marie through a mouthful of pins, 'but it's only a matter of time. They've both asked me to Simon Brown's party and I've said yes.'

'Yes to both of them?' I said.

Some people have all the luck, and then they squander it. I wouldn't mind if there was a chance that one or both of them turned round after chucking Marie at the party and decided to go out with me instead. I just knew it would never happen. When Marie was anywhere about, no boy would look anywhere else. But even if she was out of the room and I was in there, they wouldn't look at me instead. I might just as well not be there.

It was all very well for Mum to tell me to have plenty of bright conversation, to be an interesting person. They didn't seem to mind *talking* to me. But that wasn't quite what I wanted.

'I'm tired of both of them,' said Marie, unpinning the paper from me and laying it carefully on the floor. 'Right. That'll do. In fact, I'm so tired of them I don't really know why I'm hurrying with your pattern so that I can be ready on time. Les won't be.'

'Careful,' I warned. 'You'll end up as an old-fashioned, downtrodden woman, putting up with lateness and all that.'

'That's just the point,' said Marie. 'I'm not. I've told both of them I need to be free, to have no strings attached. Oh, yes, they both say, no strings. Well, this will just test it out, won't it?'

'How do you find time, apart from anything else?' I said. It seemed to me there was never enough time to do anything let alone have two boyfriends. I mean, it has always worried me that when I do (or *if* I do) have a boyfriend, when would I find time to fit him in with my life? There's ballet, orchestra, practising, as well as ordinary things like homework and our household work-sharing.

Marie had caught on to my point straight away. 'I have an old-fashioned, downtrodden mother whom I take shameless advantage of,' she said. 'On the other hand, I'm definitely *not* going to be one of them, which is another reason for not letting any of my boyfriends push me around. Might as well make one's principles felt right at the beginning, don't you think?'

After she had gone, I understood how she had enough time to go out with two, or even five boys if she wanted to. That evening dragged, far worse than any evening ever had before. I worked out what I did with my life. Ballet, two evenings a week, one hour each, finishing at seven. Leaving me with two hours beforehand to do my housework which I could do easily if I wanted to, and a whole long evening afterwards. For reading, more homework, piano practice.

Groovy.

Orchestra was on Saturday mornings. I didn't practise the cello any more. There didn't seem much need. I wasn't going to do it professionally, and the orchestra pieces weren't exactly difficult. I was doing grade seven on the piano. Another hour a day used up in practising.

I realized I only went to orchestra for something to do.

I sat at the piano, searching through the music on the lid. I couldn't find anything that fitted my restless mood. Beethoven — too passionate. I hadn't any passion to match it. I needed to have some passion stirred up, instead of this empty feeling of frustration and pointlessness. Bach? Too civilized. Chopin? Too sugary. Something noisy and modern? Stravinsky? No. The discordant notes seemed to match my splintery feelings too well. I couldn't even settle to scales and exercises, which usually soothe me when I'm feeling angry or depressed. I knew there was absolutely no point in trying to play my cello.

Rick's records were blasting away as usual upstairs. I wondered if a nice bit of noisy pop would cheer me up. I thought I'd go to his room and have a bit of company. Apart from the fact that he's got the most powerful hi-fi equipment in the house and there's not much point in anyone else putting on a record at the same time. Mind you, Mum and Dad do put their feet down occasionally – he's only allowed a certain number of hours to be unsociable in.

'Rick . . .'

The room was full of boys. Rick's age boys. They were all sitting looking intense, their eyes on the volume of sound coming from the speakers. Worshipping the noise which was so loud you could almost see it in 3-D.

Ballet tomorrow. Ballet on Thursday. Orchestra on Saturday. Great. A life packed with adventure and excitement, I don't think.

I went to bed with a very soggy book, and tried to skulk down Florentine alleys with the heroine. I almost succeeded, before I went to sleep.

The mood of depression stayed with me all week. There must be something wrong with me, I thought, if none of these boys seem to notice I'm here. If it wasn't my height, and I had to be honest enough to know that it couldn't be that really, then what was it?

Did I behave like the child people assumed I was?

I asked Marie.

'Not specially,' she said, looking at me through

narrowed eyes. 'Not so's I'd notice, anyway. But then, I'm not thinking of going out with you.'

I laughed. 'Does it make a difference?'

'I think so,' she said seriously. 'Not because of the er-um-*you*-know bit, but because they look at girls quite differently. Now I'm quite positive that both Les and Kevin look at me as a mother substitute.'

'Charming,' I said.

'So obviously you wouldn't appeal,' she went on. 'But do you really want that? I think you're better off without them.'

It was all very well for Marie, having this sort of problem. I'd just like to have the problem for a while, just to see if I could cope with it. Then I could make my own decision about whether I wanted to get rid of them or not.

We turned into her gate. It was Thursday and we were on our way home from our ballet class.

'Anyway,' I said. 'What do you do?'

'Do?' she said. 'I don't do anything. What do you mean? About Saturday? I'm not going to do anything.'

Fascinated though I was at the possible outcome of both Marie's boyfriends meeting on Saturday night, I was more concerned with me at the moment. 'No, I didn't mean that. You've done it. It's too late, unless one of them gets flu. Though I wish I could be there to see.'

'Sadist,' muttered Marie.

'I mean, how do you get them to come over and ask you out? Or whatever they do.'

'You don't,' said Marie. 'I don't know, really. It

seems as if it's the last thing you've thought about sometimes. It's when I don't expect it that it happens. I mean, it isn't like that Romeo and Juliet thing, you know, where they see each other across a crowded room and that's it, for ever. Not with my guys, anyway.'

I sighed deeply, and looked at my face in Marie's kitchen mirror. Wide cheeks, snub nose, hair slightly too gingery and a bit too wiry to make much of a sophisticated job of.

'Can you do anything about my hair?' I said hopelessly.

'Apart from dye it green?'

I cheered up. '*What* a nice thought. But they wouldn't like it at school, would they? I'd have to wear a wig.'

'Why not have a green wig?' said Marie. 'What else could we do with it, a million little plaits?'

'Reggae, you mean? They look marvellous on the right people, but do you think they'd look right on me?'

'Probably not,' said Marie. 'Okay, let me think. How about wound round the top of your head, sort of Victorian?'

'*No*,' I said. 'However charming. I'm trying to look *older*, and definitely not sweetly pretty.'

'I didn't say it wouldn't make you older. Want me to experiment?'

'You're not going anywhere tonight?' I said sarcastically.

'I don't *always* go out,' said Marie, mock huffy.

'You could have fooled me. All right. Yes. Do what you can. Only remember, whatever you do with my face and hair, there's still the rest of me underneath.'

'Next time you go out, wear your highest heels,' said Marie seriously. 'Honestly, Ros, you look marvellous in them.'

'All right,' I groaned. 'I shall cripple myself if you think I must.'

'And if you go to a disco, sit down as much as you can, then you'll win on both counts. They don't see how small you are, and you won't have to walk on your high heels.'

We went on to talk about other things, like homework, the film we'd both seen on TV last night, and whether Aileen would go back with the boy she'd been going out with since before Christmas, while Marie swept a comb through my thick hair and anchored millions of hairpins into it.

'Looks wonderful,' I had to admit when she brought the mirror across. I moved my head a bit too jerkily and half a hundredweight of hairpins fell out.

'Oh well, one tries,' said Marie.

'Would it go like that if I washed it and pinned it up wet?' I said, having taken quite a fancy to my hair like that, all bundled up on top and sticking out in an amazing way like a scruffy waterfall.

'All it needs really is a good rubber band, only I don't happen to have one,' said Marie. 'Then you wouldn't need so many hairpins.'

'Pity I haven't got a party to go to,' I said. 'Then I could wear it up for that.'

'I don't think I'm really looking forward to this party at all, after all,' said Marie. 'Somehow I think even I have gone a bit too far this time.'

Saturday, as usual, was orchestra. It hadn't occurred to me to do my hair the way Marie suggested, or to wear my high heels. I mean, I was going to orchestra, which I did every week, and everyone was used to the way I looked and probably wouldn't even notice if I *had* dyed my hair green.

So it was even more of a surprise when he asked me out.

I'd better start at the beginning. I sit at the back of the cellos. I don't mind. I prefer it that way. And whoever suggested I should learn the cello ought to have had his head examined because small fingers don't fit on a cello fingerboard any better than they would a double bass. Only nobody thought of that at the time. Which is probably a reason why I haven't taken up music as a career. Anyway, I'm quite happy, as I said, sitting sawing away and leaving out the notes I can't stretch to. It's something to do.

Behind the cellos are some of the brass section. Which always makes us annoyed because they blast holes in your eardrums on purpose when there are loud passages, and they will empty the spit from their instruments in a disgusting way on the floor behind us. Apart from that, we're quite friendly towards them, in a mock insulting way. There's this trumpet player called Barry, and we always make jokes about other people during the breaks. It's a way of covering up our own mistakes.

'Are you doing anything tonight?' he said.

I was so surprised I hadn't a clue what to say. I felt my face go all pink, and was suddenly, appallingly, conscious of my hair scraped in a bunch of unkempt strands at the back of my neck, and of my jeans which ought to have been washed but which I'd rescued from the pile because I hadn't anything else quick and easy to put on this morning.

'Er – no. Why?'

Barry twiddled the valves in his trumpet. He was standing right next to me, and I suddenly felt tall.

'There's a party – don't know whether you know him – Simon Brown. I wondered if you'd like to come.'

I hadn't asked Marie what you were supposed to say when people asked you out. I hadn't got that far.

'Well, if there's no one else,' I said flippantly.

'You haven't already been asked?' He sounded almost belligerent, as if he was daring me to say I might prefer to go with someone other than him.

'No,' I said. I could, then, have told him about Marie and her two boyfriends and how I'd go with him if only to watch the fireworks. But although we'd been laughing and bantering only a few moments ago everything seemed to be different.

Is this what it was like? I wasn't even sure whether I wanted to go. It wasn't as if I actually fancied him. He wasn't one of the guys I'd always mooned over.

Like Marie said, it came on you when you weren't looking.

Chapter 3

I phoned her when I got home.

'What do I wear?'

'What I told you on Thursday,' she said practically. 'High heels.'

I began to laugh. 'I can't,' I giggled. 'I'd tower over him.'

'Really?' said Marie.

'Well, almost. I'm sure he only asked me because. . .'

'Now stop thinking like that,' said Marie sternly. 'Shall I come over?'

'But aren't you . . . ?'

'Not really,' she said. 'If you're expecting to lose both guys at one fell swoop you're not bothered about looking really nice for it. And if by some faint mischance they don't fall out with me or behave the way I'm expecting them to, then I won't care about what I'm wearing because they'll only care for *me*. God, sounds like a bad novel, doesn't it?'

'See you soon, then,' I said, and went off to wash my hair.

I suddenly thought, as I was under the shower head, rinsing the shampoo out, that I was a bit daft making all this effort for someone I didn't really like all that much. But then, I'd been complaining that no one ever asked me out, so I suppose it was a duty, almost, to behave as if someone had, at last, even if I didn't particularly like him in that way.

'What's he like?' said Marie after we'd made coffee for Mum and Dad and gone up with ours to my bedroom.

'Short,' I said ruefully.

'Well, you can't have everything,' said Marie. 'Why haven't you told me about him before? All this whining about not knowing any boys!'

'I didn't,' I said. 'That is, he was just a sort of friend, at orchestra. Not a boyfriend, if you see what I mean.'

'I think so,' said Marie, giving me a sideways look. 'Okay, hair like yesterday?'

'Shouldn't I put my top on first? In case my hair-do gets squashed?'

'That can only improve it,' said Marie. 'You don't want to go looking well-groomed or anything. It gives people entirely the wrong idea. Those jeans you've got on, with a nice top.'

'But they're *filthy*!' I wailed.

'So much the better,' said Marie. 'Honestly, Ros, it's what everyone else will be wearing. You wear the smart stuff for night clubs, discos, things like that. But not for parties like Simon Brown's.'

'Oh, well, you would know,' I conceded, and let her get on with my hairstyle.

'You're not going out like that!' shrieked my mother when I came downstairs to show her.

'Don't be so conventional, Mum,' I said, secure in the knowledge that what Marie said was bound to be right. 'People just don't go to parties in pretty dresses any more.'

'Well, you were the one who was making all the fuss about not having boyfriends . . .' she sniffed.

'That's probably why,' I said. 'I was trying too hard. Anyway, what do you think of my hair?'

'It was your hair I was talking about,' said my mother patiently. Dad just looked, and you could see his mind ticking away in binary systems, wondering how to programme something as random as the effect Marie had created.

Rick came by, on his way to the kitchen to do the potatoes. It was Den's turn for cooking.

'Hey, Ros, that looks great,' he said.

I suddenly began to warm towards my brother.

'Thanks,' I said. 'Want me to do the spuds?'

'But it's my turn,' he began, then, 'right on. I wanted to finish taping that track . . .'

'No,' said Mum firmly.

'But she . . .'

'She may or may not have. But I know you, Rick. I wouldn't mind if you ever returned the compliment, but I know you won't.'

'*Okay*,' said Rick, 'but you've never even tried, have you?'

He stamped into the kitchen, banging cupboard doors and turning on the tap so that it sprayed all over the tiles behind the sink.

'I wouldn't have minded,' I said. 'Can't I offer?'

'No,' said Mum. 'What time are you going out?'

I couldn't understand why she was so cross. It couldn't just be my hairstyle. However, it turned out that Rick had been bloody-minded about turning his records and tapes down this morning, sending Mum half-daft with the row, so she wasn't speaking to him and he wasn't speaking to her. I began to wonder whether the compliment about my hair was really meant – he'd probably said it just to annoy her. Oh, well. I might have known. You can't rely on brothers.

I waited for Den to say something when he came in to cook about half an hour later. He actually looked at me, but it can't have been startling enough because he didn't say anything.

I was scared to move, really, during supper, in case my hair went differently from the way Marie had arranged it, and spoiled the whole thing. I started worrying whether the old jeans were right, after all. If only I was going with Marie, who would be clad in her old jeans too, making me feel that if we were the only ones at least we'd be together. And then I started feeling annoyed at her, because it was okay for *her*, she was bent on getting rid of her two boyfriends, I was on the way to getting my first one.

So I started off in a bad temper that evening.

When Barry came for me at half-past eight I'd been waiting, bored, for the last half hour; waiting all tensed up in case Mum or Dad made some funny remark, and waiting to see what he'd say about my clothes and my hair. I mean, he'd asked me with my hair looking like it does at school by the end of the day, very ordinary and a bit straggly, and with an ordinary school sort of shirt on. Not this clingy black jumper with the v-neck which plunged a bit daringly in front. I'd never worn it before and I didn't think I'd ever wear it again. Not if I felt as conspicuous in it as I did now.

His eyes travelled down the neckline in a way I didn't like. But maybe that was my imagination.

'I'm ready,' I said, not even asking him further than the front hall.

'I brought a helmet,' he said.

It wasn't until he held it out that I realized he was dressed in full leather motor-bike gear.

'I'd better put on a coat,' I said.

'I should think so,' said Barry, looking again at my neckline so that I blushed hotly.

I shrugged on a thick jacket. Must have looked *really* fantastic with my high heels, I thought bitterly. Not to mention a great big, white helmet like a spaceman's on top.

Think on the bright side, Ros, I thought, at least you won't have to walk far in these heels.

'Ever been on a bike before?' said Barry.

'Only a push-bike,' I joked. 'Do I have to pedal?'

But the sardonic humour, which we had been using against people in the orchestra, didn't seem to be funny when it was just Barry and I. It went on like that all evening.

Marie wasn't there when we arrived, for which I was devoutly thankful. I was almost afraid she would laugh at me, for only being able to attract a person like Barry. It didn't occur to me that she might have felt the same: I just assumed that she liked both Les and Kevin. Enough to have gone out with both of them at the same time anyway, even if she was intending to get rid of both of them tonight.

But being with Barry, I saw all the other blokes there in a rather rosy light. Marie had said she would meet Les and Kevin there. (At least it saved one of them being jealous of the other afterwards, I suppose.) Les was tall, dark-haired, with lovely soft brown eyes. I thought he was rather nice, myself. I certainly wouldn't have diced with his affections the way Marie was going to, I thought.

'Well, let's get ourselves a drink, then,' said Barry impatiently, as I stood rather gormlessly at the edge of the room. I saw another couple come in, waving bottles at their host.

'Shouldn't we have brought a bottle?' I said. Why hadn't Marie said?

'What? And have everyone else drink it? No, begin as you mean to go on and drink other people's, I say,' said Barry.

I was a bit shocked at this. But there was nothing I could do about it.

'What's your poison, then?' he said, setting a course directly across the room. 'Beer, wine or cider?'

'Only orange juice, please,' I said, as he turned to see if I was following and grabbed my arm to pull me along quicker. He made straight for the kitchen. It was obvious he had been here before.

'Oh, no,' groaned Barry. 'Don't tell me I've landed myself with the only girl in the district who doesn't drink!'

'Does it matter?' I said stiffly. 'I'm not stopping *you*.'

'That's not the point,' said Barry, but didn't say what the point was. He knew several of the people already in the kitchen, standing laughing loudly round a table already wet with the dribbles from unsteadily held glasses. If this was what it was like so early, what was it going to be like later on?

I watched Barry choose the largest glass he could find and fill it to the brim with beer. He tipped it up and slid the whole lot down his throat before choosing a smaller glass and saying, 'This woman only wants orange squash! Does Simon run to that sort of stuff?'

'Shouldn't think so,' said a fair boy I thought I recognized from somewhere at school. 'Not at *Simon's* parties!'

'It'll have to be water,' said Barry, 'unless your majesty deigns to drink some of this. Sweet cider. That do?'

'Only a little bit, then,' I said. I did quite like cider, but too much of it made me feel sick. I was beginning to feel too hot already, and fed up with these blokes who were now trying to see who could down their drink fastest. It wasn't that I was a prude about drink, but I couldn't see the point in tipping it down just to see how much you could take, and I genuinely didn't want any alcohol at that moment.

'Shall we see if Marie's got here yet?' I suggested, pulling tentatively at Barry's elbow after he had finished his second glassful.

'Who's Marie?'

'My best friend,' I told him. 'Shall we go through and join the others?'

'What's wrong with my friends?' said Barry belligerently, waving an arm at the blokes still shouting round the table.

'Perhaps they'll come through, if you do,' I said.

'They're only here for the beer!' said Barry, and laughed loudly. 'Okay, sunshine, hang on while I fill this up and we'll go and have a bit of a prance around.'

Someone had neglected to tell Barry the right way to talk to a girl, I thought, clasping my hardly tasted glass of cider and following Barry as – his glass refilled – he extricated himself from his drinking mates and pushed through the crush which, by now, was quite dense.

With relief I spotted Marie in the distance. Without even thinking of Barry I made my way across the room to her.

'Well?' I said.

'I've only just arrived,' she said, 'give me a chance. Actually they're both behaving very well at the moment. I might even have to give them the push myself.'

'Why?' I said, envying her. 'They're both very nice.' I could see Kevin, coming across the room towards us, as if he'd only just noticed her. Kevin was quite the opposite of Les – a skinny, blond, punky sort of boy, with startling blue eyes and a wide smile.

'I'll go,' I said. 'Barry looked a bit sulky when I came over here.'

'Why?' said Marie. 'There's nothing stopping him

from coming over as well, is there? The more the merrier.'

'Yes, well,' I said, hastily moving away. I didn't really want to be in the thick of it when the row started. Being with a sulky Barry was marginally better than that. I know I'd said I wanted to watch the fireworks, but from a safe distance. And now I felt a bit ashamed of wanting to see any kind of argument, especially between two nice people like Les and Kevin.

'Why did you run away?' said Barry fiercely when I finally located him — back by the beer, of course.

'I saw Marie,' I said. 'I thought you were following me.'

'You could have made sure, couldn't you? Have another drink.'

'No thanks,' I said.

'Oh God, I'm not landed with a prude, am I? Come on, what are you afraid of?'

'I'm not afraid,' I said. 'I just don't want any more just now, thank you.'

It wasn't true. I was a bit afraid of the way Barry was behaving. It seemed to me that I'd need to keep my cool, just in case.

Barry glared at me and finished his glassful.

'Shall we go and dance?' I suggested. The tape recorder was on at a nice loud level, not like Rick's at home, when you can't hear yourself think, but enough to make the beat really great, pounding through your feet so that they could almost dance by themselves.

'I don't dance,' said Barry.

35

'How about trying, just for once?' I said.

'I said I don't dance,' Barry repeated.

'Oh, come on.'

He tipped even more beer down his throat and turned round. 'I'm no good at it,' he stated.

'So what? We're not giving an exhibition are we? Let's go and enjoy ourselves.'

'I am enjoying myself,' he said flatly.

You could have fooled me, I thought. But I was beginning to feel annoyed with him. If he didn't want to dance, or do anything except drink, why had he bothered to ask me to this party? I had another try.

'Well, I'm not,' I said. 'I want to dance. Mind if I dance with someone else, then?'

That did it. It did it in more ways than one. He took hold of my arm, rather painfully, and steered me grimly through to the big room where at least half the guests were packed close together, wriggling their hips where there was room, just shifting weight from one foot to the other where there wasn't.

There was a space by the empty fireplace. Barry shoved me into it, dropped my arm and began to sway. I closed my eyes. I loved the feel of dancing, whether it was ballet or any modern party dance you care to name. I think, not to be too modest, I was quite good at it. The music seemed to make my body form shapes which felt great.

I didn't blame him for what he did, really, when the clear voice of one of Barry's drinking mates carried across a quiet interval between two songs.

'Hey, Barry, you look like a couple of dwarfs!'

You could almost hear him sizzle. Suddenly he looked grotesque, though he wasn't at all really. His head, with the thick mat of curly black hair on top, seemed too big for his body, and his powerful arms dangled, gorilla-like, ready to strike. Then he seemed to control himself, grabbed my arm with a claw-like fist, and hauled me out of the room.

'My coat,' I said, trying to calm him down.

Furiously silent, he gave me a look that could kill, went back inside and tore my coat and the two helmets from the heap in the hall, hurled mine at me, and kicked the bike into action.

'Get on,' he said.

'Are you all right?' I said.

It was the wrong thing to say.

'Get *on*!'

Silently I did as he said, and almost before my feet were on the footrests the bike had moved away, skidding fans of gravel out into the road.

It was exhilarating. It would have been better if I hadn't been so afraid. I didn't know how much Barry had had to drink, or how he could hold it. I didn't know him at all, I realized, in spite of those mornings at orchestra.

He drove like a maniac. Not just fast. The bike swerved this way and that, as if he was trying to shake me off. I shut my eyes and held on grimly. It was slightly better that way, though I began to feel a bit sick.

37

Street lights flashed red through my closed lids. The stink of petrol rushed into my nose. I felt the roar of the bike through my legs.

Then there was just noise, and vibration.

I opened my eyes.

We were out in the country. The road ahead was empty, and we were swallowing it up in great strips.

Little Barry, I realized, was being big.

But after a while I began to feel frightened again. He seemed to have got over his rage, and now was playing about with the bike. I didn't feel safe at all. He would accelerate forwards suddenly, then slow down, so that first I almost slid off the back, then I crashed into his back, banging the helmet on his leather collar. Then, without stopping, he went on again, swerving from one side of the road to the other and roaring round corners speedway style, lying almost flat on the road.

'Barry! Stop!' I screamed.

He stopped.

My face plate collided with his back again and my feet slipped off the rubber foot grips.

He yelled something through the helmet.

'What?'

I still had the throb of the engine in my ears, and my legs were shaking.

'You want to stop here?'

I wanted, desperately, to stop. But not here, not with Barry. I wanted him to stop somewhere safe, with hundreds of people around.

I gritted my teeth and grinned at him.

'Marvellous. Can you go that fast back?'

I didn't trust him. All the things that you read in the papers, all the things your mother tells you, in a round-about way, to be careful of since you were first a teenager, all these things swept through my mind. It says something for the way I felt about Barry at that moment that I'd rather ride dangerously on the back of his bike than be alone with him out in the country.

'All right. Hold tight.' And he sped off again.

I was more scared of him because he'd reacted so violently to the small cutting remark at the party. I mean, I know I get upset at that sort of thing, but not to the point of suicidal mania. Of course, he was pretty drunk as well.

Well, at least I'd avoided a fate worse than death, I thought almost hysterically, shutting my eyes again so that I couldn't see how fast I was going. Though, when he did another turn, grazing my feet on the road, I wondered whether we'd ever come up again and began to think that the fate worse than death might be better than death after all.

It was all over.

At our front gate I was so relieved to be there that I almost thought it had been fun. Barry parked the bike and pulled me into the bushes.

'Thanks,' I said unsteadily.

'You should have stopped out there,' said Barry. His voice sounded normal now, and I took off the helmet, able to smile and say lightly, 'Why?'

He ripped off his own helmet and said, 'Because . . . .' and kissed me.

I suppose I knew it was going to happen, and in spite

of the fact that I didn't want him to I felt a tingling down my body which was something quite new, and rather nice.

The helmets fell with a double thump to the ground. I heard one roll away to the side, under the rhododendrons.

It's wonderful what the imagination can do. I shut my eyes and thought of myself as five foot six inches tall. The man kissing me was about an inch taller – and I still had on my highest heels. I melted into his arms.

Then I opened my eyes and found the gatepost unromantically at my eye level.

No, I wasn't Marie Johnson and Barry wasn't one of my heroes. I could smell the beer on his breath and it was definitely not romantic. So much for imagination.

'Sorry, Barry, I've got to go,' I said, trying to ease myself from his clinging arms.

'A bit longer,' he said thickly.

'No, I really must go. We can't stand here – Mum and Dad will hear.'

'I said we should have stayed out there in the country. Want to go back?'

'No, Barry. Can't you understand? I want to go in now.'

He pulled his head back. 'Don't be silly,' he said. 'You're enjoying it.'

How big-headed can people get!

'Sorry,' I said, 'but no.'

Okay, Marie, you couldn't advise me on how to *get* boyfriends, but with your vast experience, tell me how you get rid of them without being really rude.

'That's what they all say,' said Barry confidently. 'When a woman says no, she always means yes.'

'What comic strips have you been reading?' I asked coldly. 'Barry, I want to go home. All right?'

'God, you women . . . when can I see you again?'

I didn't want to say I never wanted to see him again in my life. It was going to be difficult, if I wanted to stay at orchestra. But what else could I say?

'Give me a ring,' I said hastily.

It would give me a bit longer to think what to say to him. To ask advice from Marie.

'You're nice,' he said. Rather belatedly, I thought. 'You make me feel good.'

'That's nice,' I said lamely. 'Now I really must go.'

'Phone you tomorrow, then,' he said.

'All right.'

I watched him grovel for the helmet which had slid under the dark rhododendrons. There was a dusty, sharp smell to the leaves which I had never noticed before. I watched him put on his own helmet. I heard the bike roar, and waved.

I hoped I'd never have to do any of that again.

Well, I thought, as I let myself in, he was a bit disastrous for a first boyfriend. Marie can keep them all. Unless they're a bit more reasonable when they're bigger.

But all those other blokes in Simon's kitchen *were* bigger, and they were behaving exactly the same as Barry. Maybe they didn't have chips on their shoulders about being too small, like I had and obviously Barry had, but they weren't what I thought of as people it would be nice to go out with.

So much for philosophy.

I walked inside, and Den turned at the bottom of the stairs.

'Hey, I like your hairstyle,' he said.

I looked at myself in the hallstand mirror.

Marie's careful bunching up of my hair on top of my head was completely flat. Wisps straggled down my face and I had a red rim on my forehead where the skid helmet had pressed into it.

'Thanks a bunch,' I said.

Mum and Dad didn't, to give them credit, say anything at all.

I'd been dreading anyone asking me how I'd got on. They must have heard the motor bike roar up outside and stop. And they'd have counted the minutes between that and hearing it go away again, coinciding with me coming in the front door.

Well at least the minutes in between couldn't have added up to very much, so I wouldn't get any jokes about snogging on the doormat.

Rick passed me at the bottom of the stairs as he came to put out the milk bottles and I was on my way up to change out of my high heels.

'Good party?'

'No. Terrible.'

'Oh, well.'

And that was that.

I suppose I felt sorry for Barry in a way, because I was convinced he was like that because he was short. And I remember someone at school saying that

Napoleon was only aggressive because he was short. Our fourth-year history teacher, in fact.

I'd better watch it. Just in case it happens to me. Though I suppose it's easier for girls – they're not expected to be big, beefy and macho, even if it would be useful to be tall and willowy and be able to see over other people's heads in the cinema.

Talking of which, Marie and I went to see a film the next Monday evening. It was a sort of consolation for the events of Saturday.

She had telephoned me on Sunday afternoon.

'You missed it all,' she said.

'Was there a punch up?' I asked.

Marie sighed at the other end of the wire, then laughed. 'No,' she said. 'Honestly, Ros, I almost wish there had been. They were so damned *civilized* that they were almost begging each other to carry on, they didn't mind! Have you ever felt like an unwanted parcel?'

'Yes,' I said ruefully, thinking of Barry's beer glass. He certainly seemed to have had some difficulty deciding which he preferred, me or it.

'So I decided if neither of them were that worried about it, I wasn't in the slightest bit worried about either of them. Which leaves me nice and free. There's a good film on this week and I'm rather looking forward to the idea of seeing the film straight on instead of past someone's slobbery mouth. Want to come? Half price on Mondays.'

'And never much homework,' I said. 'Great.'

'What about . . . '

'Barry? I didn't really fancy him. Too short.'

'Poor thing,' said Marie, and I knew she'd want me to amplify my statement later.

'Oh, it probably isn't that he's small at all,' I said as we were waiting for the bus to town. 'Only he seems to mind so much about it.'

Her eyebrows quirked.

'All right,' I said. 'I'm sorry. I go on about it too much. I'll stop, if that's what it does to you.'

The bus came, and we went upstairs to sit amongst the stale cigarette smoke.

'And what about him?'

'Didn't you see him at the party? He never had his nose out of a glass of beer. And the more he drank the more aggressive he got. I told him to give me a ring. What do I do if he does?'

'I don't know,' said Marie. 'What do you want to do?'

'Give him the push,' I said immediately. 'Honestly, Marie, he's horrible. And the trouble is he's at orchestra on Saturdays. I shall hate going now.'

'In that case you've got to say no, but nicely. I mean, if you weren't going to see him ever in your life again you could just say exactly what you want, with no frills. But I do see . . . '

'I mean, I'm not going to go on about how I would really like to . . . but owing to pressure of work and all that . . . '

'Heavens, no,' said Marie. 'They always talk you out of that one. They never seem to have any sensitivity. Big headed, the lot of them. Think you really mean it.'

'Do you know what he said? When I said "no" . . . '

'I won't ask you what to,' giggled Marie.

'He said, "Oh, you really mean yes, women always do."!'

'Makes you wonder where they get their ideas from, doesn't it? Okay, what do you say to someone who could make your life hell if you were rude but who's too thick-skinned to understand a tactful refusal?'

'That's what I'm asking *you*.'

'Sorry, Barry, but I don't think I'm ready to go out with boys yet.'

'He might agree with me,' I grimaced.

'And then let him see you out with someone else.'

'I should be so lucky,' I laughed.

It was our stop. It was a good film, in spite of the yells and catcalls from the young kids in there. And we'd deliberately gone to the late performance because the young yobbos usually go about four o'clock, after school.

As we came out a tall, thin, clever-looking bloke stopped and said, 'Hello Marie.'

'Mark!' said Marie. 'Hi. Have you just been to this film?'

'Terrible, wasn't it?'

Neither of us answered. I didn't know whether Marie felt she oughtn't to have enjoyed it because he didn't, but I certainly did.

He was really fantastic. He made my stomach go all squiggly. Not that it mattered. I'd fallen for people before, and nothing had ever come of it. That was the story of Rosalind James's life.

45

But I was seventeen now. I had been out with someone, even if . . .

I casually shoved my elbow in Marie's side.

'Oh,' she said belatedly, 'this is my friend, Ros. Do you remember her?'

'Ros? No, I don't think I do.' He peered at me through his glasses. He looked amazingly clever, but not in the usual half-baked way of the blokes in the sixth form at school.

I was desperately trying to think where I ought to remember him from. *Had* I ever seen him before? Marie seemed to think . . .

'Mark used to be in VJ,' explained Marie before I had to make any more brain-stopping conjectures. '*And* he's brilliantly clever and never got into any of the sets we were in.'

'Poor thing,' I said flippantly. 'You missed out on a great social life, up there with the hard-working mob!'

'I know,' said Mark seriously. 'That's why I got out and went to college instead. It's much more civilized.'

'I'll bet,' I said, really envious. 'Why didn't I go there?'

'I didn't realize you were old enough,' said Mark. Tactlessly. But I was so used to this that I honestly wasn't put off.

'Seventeen a month ago,' I said. 'Really old.'

'Honestly? I'm not seventeen 'till April,' he said. Which made him two months younger than me.

He looked years older.

'Baby,' I said, and he laughed. It made me feel really great, though I don't know why. I could have said that to anyone who was younger than me and had the same reaction but wouldn't have felt the way I felt now.

The last nagging feeling that I might say 'yes' to Barry when he phoned to ask me out disappeared. Instead I was determined to get to know this really fantastic bloke. With the thought of Mark, I could even cope with Saturdays.

Chapter 4

The only trouble was, I didn't know how to get him to ask me out.

I was lucky, I suppose. He'd begun to go round to Marie's a couple of times a week because, in spite of his intelligence, he'd failed his maths at O level and had to have it to go to university. Anyway, since Marie's father teaches maths he'd said he would give him some extra coaching.

Twice a week. On Tuesdays and Thursdays. Just when she and I go to our ballet class. And of course I always — well, I used to nearly always, but now I always — went round for a coffee afterwards before walking the rest of the way home.

And since Mark had just finished his coaching lesson about that time we all had coffee together.

To start with, I wondered if I was getting in Marie's way. Not that I'd have stopped going, even if I was, because I fancied Mark so much I was even willing to be a bit of a nuisance to my best friend. Not if she was actually going out with him, I hasten to add. I couldn't do that to my best friend.

Then Marie started going out with Les again, just because, she said, she hadn't actually had a row with him and since he'd just passed his driving test she might as well take advantage of free transport for a while.

There wasn't any competition, real or imagined, now.

This sounds as if I just went round to Marie's to gaze soulfully at Mark and hope that some chemistry would happen and he'd suddenly find me the most irresistible woman he'd ever met and carry me off into the sunset. Well, I suppose I *did* hope something like that, but as well as that he was really great to talk to. We found we both liked the same kind of music – classical, I mean, and that's quite rare because nearly everyone else only likes pop. Even Barry, in spite of playing in the orchestra, didn't seem to *like* what he was doing. Which was another reason, if I wanted one, for not wanting to go out with him again.

Marie was quite happy to listen in to our conversations over the coffee in their big kitchen, our elbows leaning on the scrubbed table as we warmed our hands on the mugs. She even joined in them sometimes, but it was mostly Mark and I who talked.

And then, one day, Marie said casually, 'Can't stay with you lot, I'm afraid. Les is taking me to a disco.'

'What, now?' I said, getting up to go.

'Well, in about half an hour. Get Mark his coffee, would you, Ros, while I go and change?'

So there we were, alone at last, as they say. Not that it made any difference, really. We just talked like we usually do, then Marie came down in her disco-going clothes, we admired her, Les rang the front door bell and she said, 'Don't rush off, Ros,' and went.

We felt rather awkward, Mark and I, sitting in someone else's kitchen, drinking someone else's coffee.

'Well, I suppose . . .' I said, getting up to go.

'Yes,' said Mark. He picked up the coffee cups and stood with them irresolutely, as if he didn't know what to do with them.

'I'll wash them up,' I said.

'No, let me,' he said. He took the mugs over to the sink and began running water. I picked up a tea towel and dried them when he had finished.

Then we both stood, and if he was feeling the same as me he must have felt pretty silly too.

'See you next Tuesday, I expect,' I said, picking up my bag of ballet gear.

'How about,' began Mark, then stopped and shuffled up his books which had been in a neat pile on the table but were now in an untidy mess.

I fiddled with the handles of my bag and hoisted it on to my shoulder.

'Er — how about coming out with me tomorrow evening,' said Mark.

'Where to?' I said, and cursed myself. If only I'd asked Marie what you answered. I mean, I knew all the

49

romantic answers, from reading books, but when a bloke says something as vague as 'How about coming out?' what did you say? And how did you say it?

'Oh – the – er – cinema?' he said. Then laughed. 'No, wait a minute. I don't know why I think guys ought to ask girls to the cinema! I'd really like to go to the concert that's on at the Civic Hall. Would you like to come too?'

'Yes, please,' I said immediately. Then, 'Who's playing what?'

'You're supposed to ask that first!' teased Mark. 'Beethoven's fifth piano concerto, and some Tchaikovsky. It was the concerto I really wanted to hear.'

'Right,' I said. 'Do we need tickets or . . .'

Mark blushed. 'I've got two,' he said.

Again I needed Marie's advice. Was I supposed to offer to pay for mine? But if he'd already bought two, perhaps there was someone else he'd wanted to ask, and she couldn't or wouldn't . . .

'Thanks, I'd love to,' I said. Even if it was only because I really do like concerts, whoever asked me. It was only when we'd packed up our things, said goodnight to Mr and Mrs Johnson, and let ourselves out of the front door, that I said curiously, 'If I'd said yes I wanted to go to the cinema, what would you have done with the concert tickets?'

Mark laughed sheepishly. 'I suppose I'd have tried to talk you round. I really don't know why I said cinema, because I'd meant to ask you to the concert all the time.'

I felt warmed, wanted. It was a wonderful feeling.

And I really enjoyed the concert. The other girls at

school thought it was a terribly highbrow thing to do, but I didn't care. I'd much rather go somewhere like that with Mark than to a disco or party with anyone else.

Like Barry.

He didn't seem to want to give up.

'See you afterwards,' he said during the break in rehearsal on Saturday. This was after about three weeks of staring crossly at me and not saying anything at all.

'What for?' I said flippantly, trying to pretend I didn't know.

'See you home,' said Barry.

'I – er – ' I began.

'Oh, come on,' he said impatiently. 'Don't start that sort of thing. Be honest.'

'All right,' I said, stung into not being polite. 'No, thanks. I don't want to be seen home. I can manage by myself.'

He caught my arm as I went back to my cello. 'Oh, come on, Ros, you know you want to. Is it because I've been a bit miserable the last few weeks? I know I said I'd phone, but . . . '

'No, thanks,' I said.

'Oh, come on, don't get huffy just because I didn't get round to phoning you. I mean, I had to sort myself out.'

'It's not that,' I said, quite nicely, I thought. 'I just don't want to be seen home, thank you.'

People were beginning to look at us. I tried to get his hand off my arm, without actually shaking it and showing we were having a row. It wasn't possible.

Suddenly he let go. 'You'll come round,' he said.

I really don't know how some guys manage to be so thick skinned! I was shaking when I got back to my cello, and couldn't tune it properly because I kept turning the pegs too far. I cursed the fact that it took so long to pack it up at the end of rehearsal. I'd like to have had a violin and just have thrown it in its case and run, but my cello has a canvas bag which takes a bit of wriggling to get on, not to mention having to poke the bow down a pocket on one side and the music in a pocket at the back.

He was still waiting at the door.

'Look, Barry, I'm sorry but I really would rather go home on my own,' I said.

'You're a nice girl, Ros, but you're really slow,' he said. There was no doubt what he meant. 'You'll never get anyone if you're like that. Grow up, eh?'

He might have said that to any other girl who refused to be slobbered over in the way Barry wanted, but for me, so sensitive about my height and the way people treated me as too young, it was the last straw. If I'd had any intention of going out with him again, I didn't now. I was absolutely furious.

'I'm old enough to know what I want and what I don't want,' I said to him. 'Just because I'm small doesn't mean I m stupid, though I can see how *you* might have thought so.' I looked meaningfully at him, hoping he'd take the point.

He didn't. He was too big-headed even for that.

'You'll change your mind,' he said again, and walked away.

It was a good thing there was Mark or I might have

been really miserable. I might have gone on going out with him, confirming his belief that all the rubbish about women saying 'no' when they meant 'yes' was actually true, and not being able to get away from him because I thought I could only attract small blokes and there would never be another chance.

Yes, thank heavens for Mark, I thought.

It was going to go on, wasn't it? I hadn't heard from him since the concert, and that sweet, gentle kiss he had given me at the gate before I went in. How strangely fragrant the rhododendrons had smelled that evening, leaving a tingle in the back of my nose. I saw in the morning that the first flowers had come out the day before. I felt as if they'd bloomed especially for me, and Mark.

I was scared to go round to Marie's after ballet on Tuesday, in case he was there and didn't want to be reminded that he had taken me out last week. Unlike Barry, he hadn't promised to phone, but he hadn't been in touch with me since then either. I told myself I was being stupid, but the more I thought about it the more Barry's words rang in my brain. Was I really slow? Should I have been a bit more ardent when he kissed me? It was wonderful. Only I didn't know how to respond. I thought if I put my arms round him he might think I was too forward. You know how boys go on about girls who they don't respect. They call them 'slags' who will 'go anywhere'. I wasn't sure just what a slag was, or how you had to behave to be called one, but I didn't want Mark to think of me in the wrong way.

'Coming round for coffee?' said Marie casually

when we were changing in the smelly little room after our class.

My heart jumped. She didn't say it any differently from the way she normally does, but somehow it seemed full of enormous significance.

'Why not?' I said, but my heart was thumping. If Mark was there, I just didn't know how I was going to speak to him.

He was, and it wasn't difficult at all. I don't know why I thought it would be. He and Marie just started up an ordinary conversation, and I joined in, and that was that. And then it was time I went home, and he hadn't said anything to make me think that he still wanted to go out with me, and he didn't move his chair when I said goodbye. I heard him laugh at something Marie said, away at the back of the house, when I went out at the front.

I could have cried!

It just wasn't fair. She had two boyfriends already. She didn't need to stay and talk to Mark all evening.

I kept telling myself that he was only there for his maths coaching, but when I got home and Mum said 'How's Marie?' it was as much as I could do to mutter reply before I rushed upstairs and locked myself my room for a good weep.

Stupid, really. Because the next day there phone call.

'It's for you, titch,' said my dear brother. smallest one, too. There's something very unfair about genes, the way they've made my two brothers into ta slim blokes and me into a squat person who can't p on a pound in weight without it looking as if I'm as fat as a carthorse.

'Think how silly it would look if you were tall and we were short,' said Den when I'd complained bitterly about this one day.

'Well, exactly,' I said. 'It would suit your station in life as a young brother. As it is, you're both far too big and bossy.'

'*Bossy!*' yelled Rick. 'Hear her, Mum? She says *we're* bossy!'

Mum just smiled and let us get on with it. She never takes sides, if she can help it, which must be pretty difficult at times. I mean, she'll only take sides if the boys haven't done something they should have done, but not about things like height or intelligence or anything like that.

'Me?' I said, answering Den about the telephone. 'Who is it?'

'Some guy called Mark,' he said, disinterested.

He'd be asking for Marie's phone number or something.

'Ros? I've got a couple of tickets for the cinema tonight. *Safe Harbour*. Would you like to come?'

It was a thriller that everyone was talking about. I did want to see it. Everybody else was going to see it. And by the time it came out on video or TV you wouldn't be interested any more.

'You don't have *tickets* for the cinema!' I said.

Oh, why can't I say the right things? Why didn't I say 'Oh, Mark, I'd adore to come to the cinema with you.'? Or even, 'Sorry, I already have a date,' which I thought feverishly in bed later that I should have done, in case he thought I was too easy.

He laughed. 'They're the tickets I would have had if you hadn't wanted to come to the concert,' he said.

It *was* the right thing. It was lovely to have a private joke with a person you liked very much.

'We'd have to go on the bus, would you mind?'

Mind? After Barry's motor bike? Nobody can drive you off into the wilds on a bus.

'I'll be ready,' I promised.

And he was there, on the dot.

'I wanted to ask you when I saw you yesterday,' he said, linking my arm companionably in his as we walked up the road. My skin burned with bliss. I hardly heard his next words. 'I just thought, with Marie there, you know . . . And I couldn't even come home with you because I had to wait for her father to find this old exam paper . . . '

I understood perfectly, and squeezed his arm under mine.

I was completely happy at the bus stop. I think it was the last time I was happy like that. For a long time, at any rate.

We sat on top. I held out my fare. I didn't want him to feel he had to pay for everything. We still had bus conductors on this route, though most of them had gone. I don't know why I just didn't ask for the price of my fare. I knew what it was. But this time I had to say 'Broad Street, please.'

'Half or full fare?'

I was mortified. I could feel Mark's amusement. It

was ages since I'd had to pay adult fares. I bet if I was on a school bus and *wanted* to get half fare they'd look at me and make me pay the full one. But it had to be now, when I wanted to seem old and sophisticated and right for Mark.

I didn't dare look at him. I pretended there were amazingly interesting things out of the window. I thought if I looked at him, and he laughed at me, I'd just die. Or burst into tears. I didn't know which would be worse.

When we got off the bus I dared to look at him, and he wasn't any different from the person he had been before. He smiled at me, and squeezed my hand, and we walked along the town streets to the cinema, he helping me over the bit where they were digging up the tarmac for the new ring road, walking at an easy pace when he saw I was having to jog to keep up with his long stride.

His hand was long and thin, sort of bony, and quite dry, not like Barry's sweaty, thick fingers. I could have loved Mark just for his fingers. Then he spoiled it.

'You've got very small hands, you know.'

It was all because of that stupid conductor. No, it was all because of stupid me, asking for the road instead of just saying the price of the ticket.

I suppose if I'd made a joke of it, saying 'Why don't you try to get me in half price?' we could have laughed, and he would have seen me as an ordinary person. But I was ashamed of not looking old enough for him, and I think he felt it too.

We saw the film, and got on the bus to go home. This

time I just asked for the fare. Mark's arm crept round my shoulders. We were at the back of the bus, and there were only about three people in front, quite a long way in front.

'You're sweet, do you know that?' he murmured against my ear. 'Really cute.'

I cuddled up to him. I almost felt my knees bend upwards, though I know they didn't. I don't know why I didn't start to suck my thumb!

It was a bit of a walk from the bus stop to our house. I'd been really looking forward to that walk, in the dark as our street lights aren't very bright even when they're on. He held my hand again, and walked quite fast. I had to trot to keep up with him, especially as I'd got on my not-very-high heels and can't stride quite so fast even in them. I'm sure he did it on purpose, just so that I should have to run several steps to his one. I suppose it made him feel masterful.

'Sorry. Going too fast for you?'

'I've only got short legs,' I said, fluttering my eye-lashes up at him in the dim lamplight.

'You're a little doll,' he told me, 'really sweet. Okay, I'll slow down.'

He slowed to an almost exaggerated dawdle. It was quite difficult to walk as slowly as that, but he held me tight and our hips bumped. Or rather, his hip bumped my waist and I suppose my hip bumped his thighs. In fact, it was quite difficult to walk, full stop. So we stopped. Frequently.

His kisses were delicious, soft and nuzzling. But he had to stoop to kiss me, and it was a bit spoiled because

I felt silly at him having to bend down from his height. I tried to tell myself I was being stupid, that most men were taller than girls, and that I'd feel even sillier if I had to bend down to him.

Actually, I was quite glad we were nearly home because I'd begun to have such feelings for Mark that I was a bit frightened of them. Which came out of my inexperience, I suppose. He probably thought I'd been out with loads of boys and knew what I was doing.

The rhododendrons' perfume was heavy in the darkness. I'll never forget that scent, or the feel of their tough leaves prickling into my back, or the smell of someone's skin, next to mine.

'I'd better go in, Mark,' I whispered, scared that Mum or Dad – or worse, my brothers – might come out and see me.

'See you again?' he murmured into my neck.

'Yes,' I breathed.

'I'll phone you.'

I didn't want him to go. Not just yet. 'Do you want a coffee?' I said, still in the whispering voice, though I might as well have said it out loud.

'Better get back,' he said. 'I'll phone. Honest.'

I believed him, as I'd never believed Barry.

'Goodnight then,' I said. Although in one way I didn't want him to go, in another I was glad. I didn't think I could cope with any more emotion tonight.

I went in. Dad was having a row with Rick, who had gone to bed without putting out the milk bottles. While feeling some sympathy for Rick who had just, apparently, gone off to sleep early for the first time in weeks, and who said Dad might have given him the row in the morning, I was quite glad, because if he had come out with the bottles he'd have seen us, kissing amongst the rhododendrons, and I'd never have heard the last of it.

Chapter 5

He did phone. He was going out to the pub with some friends, and thought I'd like to go along too.

Yes, I know we shouldn't, but lots of our year do and I've only known one bloke, apart from Barry that is, who ever drinks too much and makes himself look silly. However, I didn't particularly want Mum and Dad to know, so when Mum asked me where we were going I said, 'Oh, I don't know. Out somewhere.'

'Is he nice?' she said. It was only a friendly enquiry, but I felt she was prying.

'Of course,' I snapped. 'I wouldn't go out with anybody who wasn't.'

'Very sensible,' she said, raising her eyebrows a little. 'Bring him in for coffee some time.'

'I would have,' I said, 'only he had to go, last time. It was the night Rick didn't put out the milk bottles.'

'*Which* night?' said Dad. 'He's always forgetting the milk bottles.'

'I don't know why you bother,' I said. 'Give him a different job.'

'He's got to learn his responsibilities,' said Dad with a grin. 'Sorry, Rick, even with your sister sticking up for you, you're not getting out of it.'

'Hell,' said Rick, and sloped off to his room, only to be called down immediately because it was his turn to wash up.

It sounds as if Rick was always put upon, a household drudge. It wasn't like that at all. The rest of us probably did more than he did, but he kept forgetting — accidentally or on purpose.

'All the same,' said Mum a bit later, when we were by ourselves, 'you were a bit late in, weren't you?'

'Not specially,' I said, my heart beginning to bang with indignation. Or guilt. I suppose I didn't want to think of her thinking of me in the rhododendrons, passionately kissing Mark.

'Sorry,' said Mum. 'I'd never say that to Rick, or Den. But I suppose one's daughter — and first-born! You get a bit over-protective.'

'I'm all right,' I said. I wasn't, but there was nothing my mother could do to solve my problems. In fact, I suppose I could say that it was her fault, if heredity could be a fault, that I was her height and was going to go on having problems because of it. And yet she didn't seem to have any worries about that.

'*Why* don't you mind being little?' I burst out. 'Why do you laugh at me and say it doesn't matter?'

'I suppose because I've learned that it *doesn't* matter,' she said peaceably. 'Why can't I have curly hair? Why am I fat and you're slim? Why are you good at tennis and I can't see a ball coming let alone hit it with a racquet? Stop worrying about what you haven't got, Ros, and think about what you have got! There are hundreds of people who'd give their right arms for your curly hair.'

'They can have all of it, for two more inches,' I said. 'It's worse than that, Mum, and you know it. They all treat you like a baby. Even Mark.'

'I suppose I got over that early on by being aggressive,' she said. 'You're probably too nice. Nobody dared treat me like a baby.'

'Why aggressive?' I said. 'Didn't anybody love you?'

'Oh yes, but I was brought up in the days when women were still definitely inferior to men. The women's movement had started, but it didn't affect most people. We were three sisters, as you know, and although my mother worked, my father would come home, sit by the fire, put the radio on and get waited on. I resented it, before I even thought about it. I just wouldn't accept that this was the way of things and what women just had to do. I suppose if my mother hadn't worked I wouldn't have felt it so much, but you could see her, cooking and cleaning while Dad just put his feet up. And of course we had to run round like slaves too. I wouldn't have felt it as slavery if Dad had taken his share, like your own father does. Anyway, I swore it would never happen to me, so I suppose if anyone tried the "little woman" thing on me I just exploded.'

'But Grandpa washes up now,' I objected. I was very

fond of my grandparents, who retired before I was old enough to see either of them at work.

'Oh yes, he washes up,' said Mum. She said nothing else, which in itself made me think. It was true, he did wash up, but that was about all. Yet Gran did her bit in the garden, as well as cooking, washing and cleaning for the two of them. I began to see why Mum's resentment had made her refuse to be a clinging woman.

'Don't get me wrong,' she said hastily. 'I don't think Dad knew he was being unfair. And I don't think my mother resented it. I expect she felt that if she was having her way and going out to work, then she just had to get on in her free time with the things a normal woman does. The house was never immaculate – she probably thought she was very lucky to have a husband who didn't mind.'

'Did people really do things like that?' I said, wondering. Then remembered that Marie's mother still did.

'You know they did, and do,' snapped my mother. 'Now stop whining about your size and worry about the things that are really important.'

But I didn't have all these wonderful reasons for being aggressive. Everything was about as fair as you could possibly get it in our family, even if we did moan about it. And I didn't even have to worry about the 'things' Mum thought important – like ballet, music, reading, interesting things – because we were already doing them.

I suppose the sensible thing to have done would have

been to look out for a bloke who had the qualities so admired by my mother, and me, if I'd ever thought about it. But when nobody looks at you because you look so young, you're only too glad to grab anybody who asks.

Not that Mark was like that. I was really glad to have met Mark. And it was time for him to come round and I wasn't anywhere near ready. I'd forgotten about putting on make-up, because I don't use it very often, and I still had my jeans on. I did have time to rush upstairs and change my jumper – not the black slinky thing I'd worn to go to the party with Barry in, but a soft pale green mohair. I did put on my high heels, and thought Marie was right. I'd have to buy some higher ones, even if they did cripple my feet. It was stupid standing on tiptoe to kiss your boyfriend goodnight.

'Sorry Mark, I was talking to Mum too long. Do I look all right?'

'You always look nice,' he said gallantly, and I felt reassured. If he didn't mind, I didn't see why anyone else should.

It wasn't far to the pub. His friends were already there.

'Ted, Ginny, this is Ros.'

They grinned and said hello. 'She's a little one, Mark. Which pram did you snatch her from?' joked Ted. At least, I imagine it was supposed to be a joke. Ginny, of course, was tall and had obviously taken a great deal of care with her make-up, which I should have done.

'Isn't she sweet?' said Mark. 'What do you want to drink, Ros?'

I was going to ask for wine, since we often have it at home and I like it better than beer, though Dad always offers me a glass if he's having some.

'A pint, please,' I said. 'Bitter, not lager.'

Mark's eyebrows rose. 'Fair enough,' he said. 'You don't look big enough to wrap yourself around a pint.'

I didn't feel big enough to wrap myself round a pint either, to be quite honest, but I was damned if I was going to let it stump me.

'You'd better park her in a corner where nobody can see her,' said Ted. I was beginning to dislike him. Still, I could use some of the aggression he generated in me to help.

'She'll look marvellous with a pint,' was all Mark had to say, and immediately I started feeling little and babyish when I was supposed to be feeling mature. It was as if he'd brought me here as a sort of side-show, like the bearded lady, or something.

'I can hear, you know, and understand English,' I said, a bit sharply. But Mark chose to treat that as further proof of my endearing babyishness.

The drinks arrived, and we sat down round a table – far away from the bar, just in case. But it wasn't far enough. I'd only just taken two sips from my mug when the landlord came over.

'Sorry, lads,' he said, 'but how old is your lady friend?'

He obviously wasn't talking about Ginny.

Mark looked over at me. He didn't know what to say.

'She's five,' said Ted. 'Just look at her.'

It might have been all right if Ted hadn't tried to be funny. The landlord just gave him a withering look and said directly to me, 'Well?'

'Er — seventeen,' I said. I couldn't think quickly enough to make any hedging sort of answer, and Ted had spoiled the possibility of making a joke out of it. I felt my face go hot with embarrassment.

'I'm not allowed to serve you with alcohol,' he said, 'and I'm not allowed to sell it to your friends on your behalf. So if you'd like to order a soft drink . . .'

I know he was being very reasonable, that he had every right to chuck us out and even to call the police. But I could have died. You know how people say they wished the earth would open and swallow them up? I now knew how that felt. I wished I was at home, I wished I was at school, doing my least favourite lesson, I wished I was swimming the Channel, though I can't even manage a length of the swimming baths. I wished I was *anywhere* except in that pub with Ginny looking on disdainfully and Ted laughing at Mark's discomfiture, going on about his baby-snatching again.

'You can have some of mine, Ros,' said Mark when Ted had finished joking and had drained his pint.

'No, I can't,' I said. 'He'd see.'

I knew the landlord would be watching, just in case.

'Not good for you, anyway, baby,' said Ted, shaking his head.

'I love orange juice,' I said, playing along with him, I

66

could see Mark cheer up immediately when he saw I wasn't going to be a bother, and that Ted was getting on with me all right. It was just that Ginny. But you can't please everyone.

I wished Marie was here, with her no-nonsense attitude to life. And her refusal to believe I was any different from anyone else just because I was a bit shorter. I found myself flirting with the boys, playing up to their male superiority, pretending I couldn't do things and having them show me. Even Ginny started to play up to it as well.

I felt quite disgusted with myself when we went. The boys were slightly slewed, not much, but enough to make them shout a lot along the road. I wished I'd been able to drink something. There's nothing that makes you feel out of it so much as being totally sober when other people are happily influenced by drink. And they were happily drunk – not like Barry had been. I kept on being babyish for them, and even when Ted and Ginny turned off to wherever she lived and Mark and I were alone, I went on.

'You are a cuddly little thing,' said Mark by the rhododendrons.

Suddenly I'd had enough.

'Do you want a coffee?' I said. 'It's a bit cold out here.'

'But it's nice,' he protested, grabbing hold of me as I tried to lead him towards the front door. 'I want a cuddle with my little girl.'

'Please, Mark.'

'Got to go home to Mummy,' he said solemnly.

'What will Mummy say to me, then?'

'She'll say you're very, very naughty,' I chided him, still playing my role. In fact, I knew my parents were broad-minded enough not to worry if Mark had had a bit too much to drink, and would probably make him black coffee and talk pleasantly. And Mark wasn't really drunk, just happy.

'All right,' he said. 'Love some coffee.'

I opened the door and led him through to the kitchen. 'Mum? Here's Mark.'

'It's all right, Mrs James,' said Mark, sketching a bow, 'they wouldn't let her drink anyway. She's under age.'

'So I should think,' said Mum sharply, getting up from her favourite chair by the stove, which they'd put on since it was too warm for the central heating but nice to have during the cool evenings.

'But he oughtn't to have had any either,' I protested. 'He's younger than me by two months.'

'Ah, but a lady . . . ' Mark began. I'm sure it was the beer. He didn't normally talk like this.

Mum glanced over at me and grinned. She obviously knew what I was thinking. Somehow I didn't feel embarrassed that Mark was saying all the wrong things to Mum without even knowing it.

'They all go through this stage, Ros,' she said with a mock kindliness, 'most of them grow out of it.'

'What are you talking about?' said Mark in his normal voice.

'You, you nit,' I said, 'talking as if you were a Victorian papa. You don't know how funny you sound.'

He sobered up very quickly, I will say that for him. Mind, he hadn't had all that much, just two and a half pints, so I suppose he wouldn't have got sloshed with that. It was probably Ted's influence, and me playing up to this stupid babyishness he expected now.

Suddenly we were all talking about music and books and it was all right. I was myself again. Rosalind James, seventeen, liberated woman.

Dad came in from a late meeting and brought out the sherry.

'Not for him,' I said, 'he's been on the beer.'

'Good thing we've got some beer as well, then,' said Dad. 'I wouldn't like to think of Mark being sick all night because of mixing his drinks. Sherry can be a killer if you have it with anything else.'

We sat and drank happily until about midnight, when Mark said reluctantly he ought to go, since he had an essay to finish for tomorrow.

'You'll never do it now,' I said, on the way to the door.

'Easier when you've had a pint or two,' he said. 'You don't stop to think whether what you're writing is stupid.'

'I'll try that,' I said. 'Except that if it's French I'm sure I'd start making words up.'

'So what?' he said. 'Enrich the language.'

We were outside. He closed the door gently behind him. 'Sorry about that, in the pub,' he said.

'I didn't really mind,' I said. 'It was fun watching the rest of you get more and more stupid.'

'We didn't, did we?' he said.

'Not really. But I suppose we won't be able to go there again.'

'I'll have to have nights out with the boys until you grow up,' he said, mock soulfully.

'Thanks a bunch,' I said. 'Can't you think of anything else to do?'

He could, and did. But when I went in I despised myself for acting up to him, for playing the baby.

I didn't see him often enough. It's awful how long a few days can seem when you're waiting for someone to phone or just waiting to see him again. And for some reason he wasn't at Marie's any more after our Tuesday ballet class.

'Where's Mark?' I said casually about a week after our pub visit.

Marie shrugged. 'Changed his day? I don't know.'

'I know this is all second nature to you,' I said, 'but do you find you don't stay you when you're out with blokes?'

'How do you mean?' said Marie.

'Oh, I don't know,' I said, suddenly too ashamed even to tell my best friend. 'What do you think of Mark?'

'He's all right,' said Marie.

'*All right*? Is that all you can say? You might say something a bit more enthusiastic about my boyfriend – only my *second* boyfriend – even if you do think he's an idiot.'

'I don't think that,' said Marie, smiling faintly. 'Sorry, Ros. Yes, he's nice.'

'Fantastic,' I corrected.

'Fantastic,' she agreed.

70

It should have been fun, this friendly arguing with each other, but there was something a bit strange about Marie lately. She wasn't – well – as outgoing as she used to be. Not with me at any rate. Perhaps she was falling in love with Les. Or Kevin. Or even somebody else.

I forgot about it when Mark rang up the next day and suggested we went out to a party on Saturday. I was getting really bored with orchestra – not because of the music, but because of Barry – so I jumped at the idea. Not that it clashed with orchestra, but I had a good excuse not to go because I would need to wash my hair and get my clothes all ready and other vitally necessary things. It wasn't a party like Simon Brown's – you had to look really good for it.

'What shall I wear?' I wailed to Marie over the phone. 'I've only got that skirt you made me and I've worn it hundreds of times already.'

'Sorry, I haven't time,' she said.

'No, I didn't mean would you make one, but can you come and see what I've got and tell me what I can wear? I've only got things that make me look frumpish or about six!'

'All right,' she said. 'And you can help me with my French homework.'

'I can't do it either,' I said.

'All right. The English, then.'

'Done,' I said.

But not even Marie could do anything about my wardrobe.

'It'll have to be the skirt you made me, then,' I said. 'There isn't anything else. The trouble with school

71

uniform is that you don't get dressed up enough at other times to practise.'

'I do,' said Marie. 'I won't stay in school clothes for a minute longer than I have to. First thing I do when I get home is chuck the lot on the floor and think myself into a different mood. I'd *loathe* to have that tie round my neck all evening.'

'I do take off the tie,' I admitted. 'I suppose I'm just lazy. I only change when I'm going out. Well, twice a week isn't bad – is it?'

'It's *very* bad,' said Marie severely. 'You ought to be ashamed of yourself. No wonder . . . ' She stopped.

'No wonder what?'

'Oh, nothing.'

That curious reserve again. Oh, well, put it down to the time of the month. We all have our problems.

We chose a blouse to go with the skirt, and decided that I'd really have to go out and buy some higher heels, only since I didn't have the money to get any in time for tonight I'd just have to wear the not-very-high ones that at least were comfortable.

'Now what about your English?' I said.

'I suppose I ought to do it myself,' sighed Marie. 'It's just this question about Lear that stumps me. I don't understand what it *means*, so I haven't a hope of answering it.'

'Oh, that. It's easy.' I explained it to her, and she sighed with relief.

'If I'd known that was all it meant I could have done it yesterday,' she said. 'But I always think they're trying to get you to see some terribly subtle point and I don't trust myself thinking it can be as simple as that.'

'I hope it is,' I said, 'because that's what I've written about.'

Then it was time for her to go, and for me to get changed.

'That friend of yours is a genius,' said Mum when I was all ready.

'Oh, tact!' I said. 'So you don't think I could have achieved this on my own?'

'You told me yourself you couldn't,' said Mum drily. 'But you do look nice. Enjoy yourself.'

'I will,' I said.

'Nice boy,' said Mum.

'Very,' I said.

'My God,' said Rick, 'where are *you* going? Buckingham Palace?'

'Very funny,' I said with dignity. 'It's my new image.'

'You needed one,' said my dear brother, and rushed back upstairs to put on a loud record.

Fortunately Mark rang the bell at this point or I might have retaliated, which wouldn't have done my new image much good. I took a hasty look at my face in the hall mirror, to satisfy myself that my lipstick was on properly, then opened the door.

'Wow!' said Mark, which was even nicer than Mum's praise. He bent down to kiss me before I could warn him about the lipstick, which I don't usually wear. 'That tastes nice as well,' he murmured, straightening up. 'But you don't look like my little Rosie any more. You've grown up.'

'Disappointed?' I said, a little crossly.

'I'll have to get used to it,' said Mark.

He either couldn't, or didn't want to, get used to it. At the party there was still that faint undercurrent that Rosie was the wee one, the childish one, and Rosie certainly behaved like it, gazing up at him adoringly, pretending I didn't know what they meant when they told jokes so that they had to explain them to me. Even, and I really blush to think of it now, talking babytalk. Yuk!

I tucked myself in to the largest armchair I could find, kicking off my shoes and curling my legs beneath me.

'I love the way you do that,' said Mark.

I snuggled further into the chair. 'Rosie wants a wee drinkie,' I lisped.

I was sick when I got home, and I don't think it was just the drink. Even his kisses hadn't seemed thrilling to me that night. I might just as well have been his younger sister, or a cousin he was fond of but no more.

On Sunday I couldn't bear sitting thinking of myself any longer. I shouted to Mum that I was going round to Marie's. I know it was a bit late — about ten, I suppose — but she never went to bed very early, nor did her parents, so no one would mind.

There were two figures just inside her gate as I got there. Stupid! How could I have assumed that she would be at home by herself? And she'd been behaving a bit strangely anyway, so it just *had* to be a new bloke. Whom she really cared about, or she'd have talked to me about him in the half-flippant, half-indulgent way she had about all the others.

This was obviously the wrong time to go round. I should have phoned. Not that it mattered much. I'd tease her at school tomorrow, though!

'I love you, Mark.'

My feet froze. I'd been about to turn and go back, but some kind of masochistic need made me stay there.

There are lots of people called Mark, I told myself. I tried to convince myself.

I couldn't help it. I had to know. I had to get close enough . . .

He moved, and there was no doubt. I knew that tall, thin frame. I knew the way he stooped, even to kiss a tall person like Marie. It was my Mark.

Chapter 6

I cried myself to sleep that night. I kept going back over our times together, the times we talked about music and books, and the times when I seemed to change my character completely and behave in that silly way. I cringed to think of it, and knew this must have been why Mark had gone off me and gone out with Marie. Only — that wouldn't have been so bad, if only he'd *really* broken it off, and *then* gone out with her. It was a betrayal, it was too awful. My best friend.

I should have known, I thought bitterly. She didn't mind running two blokes at once, so she wouldn't care about snatching a boyfriend from her best friend.

It was this that hurt most. Because I suppose I knew I wouldn't have been going out with Mark much longer. I just couldn't behave normally with him, and I couldn't see that changing.

I couldn't tell Mum. She'd say something sensible and I didn't want any sensible answers just now. I wanted someone to tell me Mark ought to be hung, drawn and quartered, and that I should personally poison Marie and then cut her up into little pieces.

How could I possibly face her at school?

I couldn't. When I saw her in the distance, my heart started beating as if I'd run a mile, and I felt all tight in my throat. She came over to me before we went into Assembly and I simply turned my head away.

She must have known. She didn't even try to come over to me again. We ignored each other all day. It was a bit difficult at lunch time, since we usually sit at the same table, but I waited until she'd gone to queue, then found some urgent excuse to go and get a new French exercise book so that she'd nearly finished by the time I carried my tray over to the seat the rest of them had saved for me. Marie got up. It was that obvious, because she hadn't finished her pudding. It was jam tart, which they do quite well at our school and which she normally loves.

'What's up with you two?' said Aileen with a raised eyebrow.

'Nothing much,' I muttered.

'Come off it,' said Dawn. 'We've been watching you all morning and there's definitely something wrong.'

'We're just not speaking, that's all,' I said.

'Why? Have you pinched one of her boyfriends?' Dawn's sleepy eyes became sharp and alert for once.

'No,' I said, too quickly.

'She's pinched one of yours?' suggested Aileen.

'Oh, shut up, all of you,' I said thickly through my teeth. 'I don't want to talk about it. All right?'

'Okay,' said Aileen, shrugging her shoulders. 'We'll have to ask Marie, that's all.'

'I don't suppose she'll say anything either,' I said fiercely, though why I thought she would have enough remnants of loyalty to keep quiet about our row when she couldn't keep her hands off Mark I don't know. I was still trying to see some good in her, in spite of everything. I might have saved myself the trouble.

It was all round our form before we went home. I kept getting sympathetic looks from across the desks during English. Most of our crowd did English, though we didn't all do the same other A levels. Oh well, charming of her to tell them. Now everyone would be laughing behind my back. Poor old Ros. First she gets a rotten boyfriend for about a week, then she gets another one which her best friend snatches from her. Not much experience. Poor old Ros. You can't blame him, really, though, can you? I could hear it all in my own imagination. I knew how they'd be talking. Well, there hadn't been much else to talk about in our form for some time.

I cried all evening when I went home. I just pretended I had stacks of homework to do and only just managed to stop crying enough to come down for supper later on. Even so, I had pretty red eyes, and I saw Mum looking anxiously at me. The boys never notice anything, thank God, so I didn't have any tactless comments from them.

And then Mark phoned.

Rick took the call and came screeching back right in the middle of Dad's Quiche Lorraine, 'It's your boyfriend!'

I couldn't say I didn't want to speak to him. I'd have to have explained, and I couldn't do that without weeping salt all over my tomato salad.

By some miracle, my voice was quite steady.

'Hello, Mark.'

'Ros. That concert on Wednesday. Shall we go?'

'No,' I said, trying to keep the tears from my voice. 'No, I don't think so, Mark.'

'Are you doing something else?' he said, sounding surprised. 'I didn't know.'

'I'm not,' I said. 'You are. Give Marie my love.'

There was a silence at the other end of the line. I should have slammed down the receiver. I don't know why I didn't. I suppose I wanted to hear from him that it wasn't true. That I'd mistaken it all. That it was another Mark, with the same back view. And that Marie only wasn't speaking to me today because she thought it was awful that her best friend could possibly think such a thing of her.

'I'm sorry,' he said after a long pause. 'Listen, Ros, I must explain . . . '

This time I did slam down the receiver.

So it was really true and the last faint hope that it wasn't died within me. I finished my supper in silence, made some kind of conversation though I haven't a clue what it was, then managed to go back upstairs where the feeling of lead in my stomach stayed for the rest of the evening, and was still there when I woke next morning.

It was a terrible week. I just couldn't concentrate on anything. I kept wanting to cry in the middle of lessons, and as for King Lear, howling his heart out because of the harshness of his own daughters, I knew just how he felt!

And still I couldn't meet Marie's eye. I knew she must despise me. If she could take Mark away from me as easily as that . . .

It was all because of my baby face, my childish, round face with the big eyes and the snub nose. It might make blokes attracted to me to begin with, but when they found I couldn't do anything normal, like everyone else, that I was asked if I wanted half fare on the bus and that I couldn't drink in the pub, it wasn't surprising that they didn't want to know any more.

Aileen and Dawn and some of the others met in a corner of our form room when they didn't think Marie or I knew. At least, I think that's what they thought because once when I came back for a book I wanted to take back to the library they stopped talking and looked round sort of guiltily. And Marie wasn't one of them. So they were talking about us. It didn't occur to me to wonder what they were saying about Marie. I only thought miserably that they'd be despising me for being so stupid.

And yet the thing I missed most was Marie's friendship.

I'd just come back from ballet on Thursday and had started crying again because she wouldn't meet my eye though I desperately wanted to talk to her. I must have looked a freak, all blotchy and puffy, though Mum still didn't say anything. I wanted to go to her and bawl, but something in me said that I'd got to face it on my own. I wasn't a baby any more, however much I looked like one.

'Ros! Telephone!'

I put down the novel I was trying to read because I couldn't concentrate on my homework and opened my bedroom door.

'Who is it?'

'Someone called Mark.' You could hear the triumph in my horrible brother's voice. He knew who Mark was all right.

'Tell him to get stuffed!' I yelled back.

'In those words?'

'If you like.'

My mother was on the landing and heard me.

'Ros, if you want to be rude, be rude in person,' she said sharply. 'Don't make someone else do it for you.'

'Sorry,' I said, though Rick said rude things to people so often I didn't think it could possibly hurt his character to do it for me. 'Okay, I'll answer it.'

Mum's sharp words did me the most good I could have wanted. I was annoyed with her for being annoyed with me, and this dried up my tears so that I was really angry by the time I got downstairs to the phone.

'Well?' I said. I didn't mean it to come out quite as peremptory as that.

'Ros?' He sounded hesitant, worried.

'I don't know how you've got the nerve,' I said, and something at the back of my mind was amazed at me. 'I don't want to talk to you, thank you.'

'Wait, Ros, you must listen.'

'Why?' I said.

'No, really, you must listen. Not for me, for Marie.'

'Why should I care about Marie?' I said stiffly, half of me wildly angry and the other half wanting desperately for him to say Marie was sorry and would let him go. And then I'd say I wouldn't take him with a box of After Eights thrown in.

'Because she's scared of you. She's your best friend . . . '

'*Was*,' I said emphatically.

'And she really cares that she's hurt you.'

'She should have thought of that before, shouldn't she?' I said nastily. 'If she cares that much why doesn't she come round and tell me herself?'

And with that I slammed down the receiver, feeling much, much better. Mum was right. It was much more satisfying to do your own dirty work. Although I don't think that was quite what she meant.

I went to school the next day determined that nobody was going to feel sorry for me. So what if a bloke preferred someone else? I didn't like him all that much anyway. Next time I'd do it first, and have the satisfaction of making someone else's life miserable.

I felt slightly ashamed of this later on, but on that Friday it was the thing that kept me going. When I caught Aileen and the rest of them gradually merging together as if they were going to have another nice discussion about me and Marie I deliberately barged in and started talking strenuously about last night's homework. Which I did in fact need some help with because I'd been so upset before that telephone call that I hadn't been able to think straight.

They told me what it was all about, and I looked at some of the text. Not that it made much difference; I still felt a bit woolly about it – then I said, 'Look, I know Marie and I have had a row. You know why we've had a row. It's all over now, and if we don't want to speak to each other that's our problem, not yours, all right?'

'What do you mean?' said Janice Elver. She would. She always manages to say the wrong thing.

'We know what she means, Jan,' said Aileen. 'Sorry, Ros. Okay?'

Which meant that they wouldn't discuss us any more. Not so obviously anyway.

I was beginning to feel a whole lot better. Perhaps having a few hammer blows was quite good for you. Not that I liked it at the time, but I was beginning to feel that I was a person who could do things for myself now. I hadn't realized how much people *treating* me as if I was much younger than I am had made me *behave* a lot younger. And I suppose you've got to come up against people like Barry at some time or another just to show that you don't want anything to do with people like Barry.

Which reminded me. It was orchestra tomorrow. Oh God, I groaned inwardly to myself. Men! Why do they make life so difficult?

I went home feeling quite cheerful, even though I'd deliberately avoided Marie again all day. I found that you didn't even have to be miles away from people you didn't want to know, you just pretended you never saw them, staring right through them as if they were ghosts. I felt her once try to make some movement towards me, but I bent my eyes to my book and she didn't, after all.

In fact, I'd emptied my mind so much of Marie that when the doorbell went that evening after supper I just happened to be nearest and went to open it.

She was on the doorstep. My stomach went right down to my knees.

'Oh. Hello. Come in.'

'I won't if you don't want me to,' said Marie, 'but I wanted to come and say sorry.'

'You'd better come in,' I said. You can't be friends with someone for years and years and then let them say sorry on the doorstep and go away again.

We sat stiffly in my room. Neither of us knew how to start.

'Want some coffee?' I said.

'Shall I make it?' said Marie, jumping up.

'Come down with me,' I said.

We couldn't talk down in the kitchen, because Dad

and Den were folding clothes ready for ironing and Mum was coming in from time to time to ask Dad's opinion about something to do with her school computer. Perhaps that was a good thing. Marie was used to the hurly burly in our house, and we started to talk about ordinary school things, in an ordinary sort of way, just like we always had before this happened.

'Shall we take it upstairs?' I said when our mugs were full. 'Can't hear yourself think among this lot.'

Marie smiled. 'Good idea,' she said.

So there we were, looking at each other again, with our mugs of coffee held nervously in our hands.

'I really am sorry,' she started, then stopped, and looked down at the bubbles on top of the brown liquid.

'You're not,' I said. 'If you were sorry you'd throw him over and say, "Here's Mark, if you'll have him." '

'As if you could trade in people like that!' said Marie in her old, scornful voice.

I laughed, and looked at her properly for the first time. 'All I want to know is, why? I mean, *why*?'

She sighed, a fluttery, sobbing sort of sigh, and looked down at her coffee again. 'I just fell for him, Ros. Honestly. I'd never felt like that about anyone at all, ever. You know that time I went out with Les to the disco, when you were still talking to Mark . . . '

I remembered.

' . . . it was just *awful*. Not that I don't like Les. I do. He's really nice. So's Kevin. So were all – or most – of the other blokes I've ever been out with. But Mark – he's so different. When he asked you to that concert –

84

Ros, I'm sorry, really I'm sorry, but I could have murdered you!'

She was really crying now, and I went over and put a hand on her shoulder.

'It's all right, Marie. I don't mind, not that much. I was just hurt, really. I didn't like him like that. In fact . . . '

She raised a tearstained face. 'Don't try to be kind, Ros,' she sniffed, 'I really couldn't bear it.'

'No, honestly. I thought he was wonderful at first. He *is* wonderful!' I said hastily, as she began to give me a mock growl through her tears. 'Hell, you can't have it both ways! It was when the conductor asked if I wanted half price on the bus . . . '

'You *what*?' said Marie, her tears finished now. She began to mop her face with an old tissue.

'It's all right for you,' I said impatiently. 'You've looked ninety since you were born . . . '

' . . . Thanks a bunch . . . '

' . . . but it seemed to happen all the *time* when I was with Mark. There was that, and not getting served a drink in the pub . . . '

'Oh, poor Ros!'

'It seemed a coincidence, but I suppose it was just because I've never wanted to go to a pub before and the bus conductor just happened to be a nice one instead of the usual crabby ones that want you to pay full fare when you're twelve. But it made Mark treat me like a sweet little thing, and I played up to it. Oh, Marie, you should have *heard* me!'

'It worried him,' said Marie. 'That's why I said you ought to bother more about clothes and that. And make-up.'

'Oh, did you mean that?' I said vaguely. I'd almost forgotten about it. 'Did he say anything? About me?'

'No,' said Marie. 'Honestly, he didn't. I was just reading between the lines. What he said to *me*. Which he probably won't any more. I'm sorry, Ros, I knew I was going to hurt you, but I just couldn't help myself. He didn't mean to two-time you. It was my fault. We'd been talking, once when he came for an extra lesson from Dad, and then my parents went out and I just knew, and . . . '

'Don't tell me, I can imagine,' I said bleakly.

'He felt awful about it, too. And he said he ought to tell you. But I said don't because I didn't want you to know it was me. I suppose I hoped he'd just break it off and you wouldn't know.'

'Yes, I would,' I said. I laughed. 'I don't seem to be doing too well, do I? Baby Face Ros, that's me. I'll probably end up the fastest gun-slinger in the West. Seriously, though, Marie, I think it's time I changed my image. Not just in a temporary way, but for good. I'm going to chuck out all that stuff in my wardrobe and go out and get something really slinky. And I don't care if I'm *crippled*, I'm going to wear the highest heels they do in size three!'

'Shall I come with you?' she said.

'Great. Haven't had a good Saturday afternoon shop for ages. After orchestra. Shall we have a hamburger in town?'

'Lovely,' said Marie. 'Nice for some to be stinking rich enough to replenish a whole wardrobe. But I'm not jealous.'

'Not a whole wardrobe, not all at once. Only this month's complete allowance.' I could afford to be generous, I thought. It must have been awful coming round like this. 'You've got something better,' I assured her.

'I didn't mean . . . ' she began.

'You did,' I said. 'Now all I need is a way of getting rid of Barry, for good and all. How do people get like that, Marie? You'd think he'd give up.'

'There you are,' said Marie, 'someone loves you, even if it's not the one you want.'

'No,' I said sadly. 'You are lucky, Marie.'

So we went into town on Saturday afternoon, and it was as if we'd never fallen out at all. And this time we bought my new shoes first and put them on to try out my new clothes. It made all the difference. Suddenly I could see what it must be like to be a couple of inches taller. It made everything look so much nicer, and I was really pleased with everything we got.

This was the start of the new Age of Ros. And I'm not joking about the age!

Chapter 7

'Can I have a word with you, Rosalind?' said Miss Libetta at the end of our ballet lesson on Tuesday.

We had given our curtseys to her and the pianist, and were about to go out in our usual straggly way. When you've been using all your muscles strenuously for an hour, with sweat dripping down your back, you don't feel like walking out in a disciplined line and Miss Libetta, thank heavens, didn't insist on it.

I waited for the odd people to make requests and pay fees, then when they'd all gone she turned to me and said, 'How do you feel about doing a little teaching?'

I didn't think I'd heard properly.

'Teaching?'

'Yes. Your technique is very solid, and you've been very good with the little ones when I've asked you to do bits of emergency work with them. The thing is, Mrs Owen is leaving at the end of this term.'

'Yes, I knew that. She's having a baby, isn't she? Nice.'

'Nice for her,' said Miss Libetta with a little grimace, 'but it leaves us in a spot. None of the advanced girls are at all interested – and besides, their most important class is on Saturday mornings. I wondered if you'd like to take over the babies' and scholars' classes for me. Possibly even the Grade I.'

I thought. It was orchestra on Saturday. I'd really like to do it, but I didn't know whether I ought to. There was the concert half-way through next term. But the thought that I wouldn't have to have Barry glowering at me . . .

'Can I think about it?' I said quickly. 'Sorry, but I'm supposed to go to orchestra on Saturdays. I don't mind missing it, but I'd better ask Mum what she thinks.'

'Of course. If you can let me know on Thursday I'd be very grateful. And then you can perhaps sit in with Mrs Owen for the last week or two of term to see what she does with the babies. Scholars' is no problem. You know that backwards, and it's just syllabus work. You'd have to use a tape, but you can probably do that better than I!'

We both laughed, because on the days when we don't have a pianist for one reason or another I always have to work the tape for her. How I was going to do that and teach at the same time, I didn't know, but no doubt Mrs Owen coped all right so there was no reason why I shouldn't.

'And of course you'd be paid the proper student-teacher rates,' she said as I was about to give another respectful curtsey and go.

'Paid?' I said. 'That's different.'

She knew I was joking really, that I'd have done it for nothing if it was all right to miss orchestra.

'It all helps,' she said.

I'd pretty well made up my mind, but I knew I'd have to ask Mum what she thought first. Not that I thought she'd think any differently from me, really.

'What was all that about?' said Marie, still waiting for me in the changing room.

'She's asked me to take over the baby classes,' I said in a kind of daze.

'Good on you,' said my friend. 'I wondered who she'd get.'

'But why me?' I protested. 'You're much better than I am.'

'I couldn't teach,' said Marie with a shudder. 'If they put one toe out of line I'd probably yell at them so that they wet their knickers or something. Now you're good with them – endless patience.'

'Probably because they're smaller than me,' I said. 'I feel in control. Anyway, I like them.'

'There you are, then,' said Marie. 'That's why you're successful. I hate the little brutes.'

'Come off it,' I said. 'You don't really.'

But I thought I really knew what it was. Perhaps there's something to be said for not being quite as good as Marie is at things. You know why other people can't do them, and can sympathize. Whereas Marie just doesn't understand why somebody else can't and she gets impatient.

We walked home together, friends again, except that at her gate I said goodbye.

'You know you can come in if you like,' said Marie hesitantly.

'What? And spoil your romance? No, thanks,' I said.

'You'd both be embarrassed and I'd probably say something rude.'

'Perhaps some time when you feel you can. Mark feels awful about it too.'

It was the first time since Friday that we'd mentioned Mark.

'Serves him right,' I said. 'I hope he feels guilty for the rest of his life. Well, for some time, anyway.'

I could joke about it now, but I knew I was going to miss Marie's company on these after-ballet evenings. I know she'd always gone out a lot before, while I sat at home and did my practising and homework, but ever since I'd had somebody to go out with too it was going to seem very empty for a while.

Come on, Ros, stop feeling sorry for yourself, I scolded myself. Marie Johnson hasn't been asked to teach the baby classes and you have.

I ran inside.

'Hey, listen, Miss Libetta's asked me to do some teaching!'

Mum turned from the television instantly.

'Ros! How lovely. What a compliment. I hope you said yes.'

'Well, the only thing is, it's Saturday morning.'

'So what?' said Den, his eyes glued to the Western.

I ignored him. 'Orchestra,' I said to Mum.

'Don't do it,' said Rick. 'I couldn't stand another teacher in the family.'

Mum gave him a smart kick on the behind as he sat on the floor by her feet. 'I'll give you an extra washing up for that, my lad,' she said. 'Yes, what will you do about orchestra? What a pity they'll clash.'

'Would it be all right if I gave it up?' I said. 'I'm not that good, and I never practise the cello now. It was just for fun, really, and it's not always fun now.' Because of Barry, I didn't say. 'And I'd get paid.'

I don't know how much Mum knew, or guessed, about Barry, but I think she understood a lot more than I gave her credit for.

'I don't think there'd be any problem. If you'd really prefer to teach, then do it. But you have to make up your own mind.'

'I have,' I said happily. 'Thanks, Mum.'

The boys went on at me all evening, of course, about being a teacher, but eventually Den went to bed and Rick wandered back upstairs to make a row on his record player and I was left with Mum and Dad, the television mercifully silent.

'What's this?' said Dad, who hadn't been in the room when I came home. 'Another teacher in the family? I couldn't bear it!'

'Oh, don't you start as well,' I grumbled, though I knew he was just teasing me. 'Mum'll give you washing up as well. But isn't it nice, Dad?'

'I'm proud of you,' was all he said, but it was enough. More than enough. Suddenly Baby Face was turning out to be a mature woman, and I thought I rather liked it.

'All I need now is a nice boyfriend,' I said, rather unguardedly, I must admit.

'I thought you had one,' said Dad, who doesn't have the same perception as Mum about some things.

'I chucked him,' I said untruthfully. 'He treated me as if I was six.'

'Oh, well, we can't have that,' he said. 'But don't grow up too soon, Ros. I feel as if I've missed you being a child, you're so grown up these days.'

'Really?' I couldn't believe it. Why don't people *tell* you, then you wouldn't go round feeling small and inadequate.

'You're the most responsible of the three of you,' he said. 'Don't overdo it – you must let Rick and Den have a chance.'

'But I do!' I protested.

'Not really,' he said. 'I'm always catching you doing the odd last saucepan for Den, or taking Mum tea when it's Rick's job. Let them get into a row, let them know they've got to do a job properly, don't let them lean on you.'

'Well, they are younger,' I said, from the security of suddenly knowing I was older.

'You did the same when you were Den's age, and the same when you were Rick's age. The curse of being the eldest, I suppose. Anyway, if you've got a job now you won't have time to do things for them. No wonder they're feeling a bit put out about it.'

'It's only Saturday mornings,' I said. 'Don't make it sound like a lifetime commitment.'

'You know what I mean,' he said. 'Now does anybody mind if I watch the snooker?'

So on Thursday I told Miss Libetta that I could do the teaching, and with some trepidation went into Mrs

Owen's first class on Saturday morning to help. Although I had helped with them before, it seemed different this time, now that I knew I'd have to do it all myself. It's easy when someone tells you what to do — like telling me to take three of the newest scholars out to the little room at the back and help them dance a polka. It was different to watch the whole thing and try to remember what order to do things in, and to think what muscles the tinies were using so that I didn't damage their feet by asking them to do the wrong things.

It wasn't as difficult as I thought it was going to be, though. When you've spent two hours a week for the last thirteen years doing the exercises, I don't think you could possibly do it wrong. But I began to understand how hard it was to teach when Mrs Owen suddenly said, 'Right, Rosalind, you take the last quarter of an hour. You've done the polka for me before. It's only that and their jumping. Shall I stay, or would you rather I went out?'

It was tactful of her, and I hesitated. Part of me wanted her there, in case I did everything wrong, but another part of me knew that I'd do it a lot better if she wasn't there.

'I'll try on my own,' I said.

'Fine. I'll go and make the coffee, then. We'll all get it a bit early today.'

To begin with I think I shouted at them a bit, because I was so nervous, but when one little girl came up to me and said, 'Please, Miss James, is it this leg or this one?' I felt suddenly that I was doing it all the wrong way.

It was that 'Miss James' that did it. Although Mrs Owen had introduced me by that name, it really didn't occur to me that the kids would actually call me that. There's nothing like having a proper title to make you feel the part!

'Let's all sort it out, step by step,' I said. 'It's not really difficult. Let me see all your right feet beautifully pointed.'

After a short delay while we sorted out which was the right foot of some of them who weren't quite sure, I explained each part of the step so that they really enjoyed it, and by the time Mrs Owen came in with two cups of coffee I was ready to put the tape on and see if they could do it to the music.

She sat down quietly in a corner while I counted them in. I could have hugged them all! There was only one small child who still couldn't do it, which Mrs Owen said was pretty good since they'd been on that step all term and only half of them had managed it up to now.

Warmed by all this praise, I finished the lesson with her watching me. And made a complete mess of it! They seemed to be falling over their feet all the time and when they had to do jumping steps they were completely out of time, bouncing up and down like adorable little rubber balls dropped at random.

However, I didn't think I'd ever be so frightened again. And when Mrs Owen had left and I was on my own I'd be able to arrange the length of time for each exercise to suit myself and my way of teaching.

'I feel like Jane Eyre, going into her first governess

job,' I told my mother when I got home at lunch time.

'How did you get on?'

'Okay, I think. I managed to teach them a step that they'd got a bit tangled up with all term, apparently.'

'The test is, will they be able to do it next week?' said Mum.

'Oh, thanks,' I said. 'Build up my confidence, won't you?'

It was nearly end of term. Everything was winding down. The Drama Club did their play and Marie and I even went to see it, paying precious money for the privilege. But it was very good, even though Alison Sinclair as the leading lady forgot her words at least seven times.

'She'll know them by Saturday,' said Marie charitably as we walked home.

'She'd better hurry up,' I said. 'She's only got tomorrow. Coming in for coffee?'

'Well,' she hesitated.

'Unless of course you're meeting Mark.'

'It's not that, it was just . . . '

'You've been here before. You've been here since,' I told her. 'So you're meeting Mark. I understand. I won't get in your way.'

'I know you won't,' said Marie. 'And yes, I suppose I am meeting Mark, that is, he'll be at home, waiting, because I didn't know what time the play would end and I didn't . . . '

' . . . want him to bump into me at school,' I finished for her.

She nodded, dumbly.

'I suppose I'll have to bump into him sometime,' I said.

'I *really* am sorry, Ros,' she said miserably.

'Look, don't spoil it just because of me,' I said impatiently. 'It's all over. Finished. And you might as well come in for a coffee even if it's for only half an hour. Let him hang about for a bit. Show him you're not running to him when he crooks his little finger.'

'*You* try being strong-minded when you feel the way I do,' said Marie ruefully. 'But you're probably right. I'll come in for half an hour. After all, he doesn't know what time it finished.'

So we spent half an hour together. It was almost like old times. But I couldn't help a nagging tinge of resentment, still in the back of my mind. Our friendship would never really be the same again, but perhaps, as we grew older, it wouldn't have been anyway.

Chapter 8

Then it was Easter. We weren't going away. Marie was. With Mark and his family.

The hidden resentment which I thought might disappear came flaring to the surface.

'What's *wrong* with you?' shouted Rick as I yelled at

him for something he hadn't done properly. 'Have you got the curse coming or something?'

Someone had recently told him about girls' periods and PMT and he now blamed every outburst of my bad temper on to it.

'You leave my PMT alone!' I yelled back. 'Can't I be angry with you just because it's your fault for once?'

'No!' he bawled. 'I just hate bad-tempered sisters.'

'How do you know?' I demanded. 'You've only got one. You can't generalize on the strength of one.'

'All my friends have got them,' said Rick, scrubbing so fiercely at the neglected worktop that I thought he'd take the complete surface off.

'Oh, great. I could equally well say that the sisters of all your friends must have a tough time because their *brothers* are so awful and useless.'

'Be quiet, both of you,' said Mum, coming in to see what the row was about. 'No, I don't want to hear. I've listened in to your quarrels so many times I know you're both to blame. Be *quiet* Rick. My goodness, I'll be glad when these holidays are over.'

And so would I, I thought. Couldn't Marie have waited until *after* the Easter holidays? Couldn't she have let me have at least *some* time with Mark before she stole him from me?

And there was no ballet, no piano lessons, no orchestra or its replacement teaching. We were all at home and the weather was vile, pouring buckets all day and every day, so that you didn't want to go out even though it might have done us a lot of good if we had.

I stayed up in my room a lot of the time, because

when I came downstairs I'd be sure to bump into Rick and we'd have a row. Den was all right, though that was probably because he was round at his friends' most of the time, and when he wasn't there his friends were at ours and they spent hours in his room, running the model railway all over his bed by the sound of it.

I wrote reams of gloomy poetry and listened to sad music on my tape recorder. I went to the library and got out even more gloomy music tapes. It was when I found I was beginning to enjoy being a tragedy queen that I saw the funny side and came downstairs and began to talk to people again. In any case, it would be school in a couple of days and I had a ton of holiday work to do.

'Trust you,' said Mum, watching me lay out books and paper on the dining-room table. 'You spend all your holiday upstairs where you could be doing your work, and when it's nearly too late you come and use up *my* space. It's because of you that my pupils don't get holiday homework from me. I know it's not worth the bother. They won't learn much in that last two hours before breakfast on the first day.'

'It's always seemed a bit pointless to me as well,' I said. 'But this,' I showed her, 'is something I should have done during last term and didn't get round to.'

Another amazing thing, I thought. Until the Mark thing, I would never have let my teacher mother know I hadn't done what I was supposed to do at school.

Encouraged by myself, I burst out, 'Marie's going out with Mark.'

'I thought something like that had happened,' said

Mum mildly. 'But you seem to be friends still.'

'It took a bit of doing,' I admitted, 'and it was mostly Marie coming round to make up. I was glad, really. But I hate her guts sometimes.'

'Bound to,' said Mum. 'But there are other fish in the sea. Don't despair for ever.'

'Oh, Mum!' I groaned. 'I thought you were the last person to say something clichéd like that! Did you have to?'

'Sorry,' grinned Mum. 'Insensitive me as usual. Blame it on term beginning and me having to think what I'm going to do with twenty brats while the other twenty are doing exams, and, last but not least, you using up my table.'

'Sorry. Point taken. I'll take it upstairs. But it won't get done so well up there.'

'Whose fault is that?' she said. 'It's been free for the past ten days.'

'Had a good time?' I said to Marie when she came to call for me on the first day of term.

'No,' said Marie.

'Oh?'

'Just rotten weather. Nothing wrong otherwise,' she said. 'But I refuse to think it's romantic having a tent leak all over you in the middle of a night during a thunderstorm. I mean, if Mark had been there with me . . . but he was over the other side of his parents' tent and though his Dad heard me yelling and came to rescue me, Mark slept through it all!'

'So much for true love!' I grinned.

'*And* they made sure he was banished to his tent and I to mine before they turned in themselves,' said Marie. 'Honestly, what did they think we'd do?'

'They'd probably be right,' I said.

'Well, yes, probably,' she said, 'but I didn't get the chance, so it was all a bit of a literal washout. How about you?'

'Boring,' I said. 'We didn't do anything except quarrel. Of course the weather would cheer up on the first day back.' I looked savagely out at the blazing sun and the cherry blossom lifting its bruised petals to the heat.

'Anyway, Easter is the most ridiculous time to go camping,' said Marie crossly as we took a short cut over the sodden playing fields of the primary school next door, which we weren't supposed to do but did when we felt particularly out of sympathy with school. 'Talking of camping, are you going to Morgan Castle?'

'Oh, lord, I'd forgotten about that. Haven't even asked Mum. I will, tonight. Are you?'

'Yes,' said Marie. 'And Mark isn't.' She looked me straight in the eye.

'He wouldn't, would he?' I said reasonably. 'It's only school, isn't it? Not college.'

'I don't know,' said Marie. 'Anyway, he isn't.'

'Okay, I'll come, so long as you promise not to telephone him every night.'

'All right,' said Marie, 'I'll phone my parents instead and make sure he's there. Anyway, you never know who you'll meet there.'

'I should be so lucky,' I said. 'I've given up the idea of

boyfriends for the moment. Anyway, I've got ballet classes to think about. Oh, no! I won't be able to go. I've got my Saturday mornings!'

'Miss Libetta's closed at half term, isn't she?'

This was true, so my momentary panic was over.

We'd been to Morgan Castle together at the end of our fourth year. It's an outdoor activities centre owned by the local authority, and you go there to do canoeing, climbing, all that sort of thing. It's in Wales, and satisfactorily far from home. We had a great time two years ago. I was looking forward to it, so long as Mum and Dad agreed to cough up the money. Even so, I thought, I had my dancing money now. I could use that.

'This time I'm going rock climbing,' I said. I'd always been fascinated by films of Himalayan expeditions, and we still had a years-old video of the climb up the stack called The Old Man of Hoy.

'You're mad,' shivered Marie. 'I get vertigo.'

'I'm not *very* keen on heights,' I said cautiously, 'but I can manage ladders to our upstairs windows.'

'I *definitely* can't,' said Marie, 'so I'm not going climbing. Do you know, once our cat got on the roof of Mackie's next door, and my parents were out but the window cleaner was around. So I grabbed his ladder and asked him to go up for poor old Puskhin, but he said I ought to because the cat knew me. Do you know, Ros, I got to the *last two steps*, I could have stretched out my arms and even got Pushky down, but I *couldn't*. I was frozen. I could only unfreeze to go down, and then my legs were shaking that much I nearly wobbled myself off the ladder!'

102

'Then what?' I asked through my giggles.

'Oh, he had to go up himself, and Pushkin scratched him to pieces. Turned out he'd got a phobia about cats about as bad as my phobia for heights, Bit unfair, really.'

'I suppose he fancied you,' I said cruelly.

'No, I don't think so,' said Marie quietly, and I felt ashamed of myself. We parted at my gate, and I went in to see if my parents were prepared to pay for another trip to Morgan Castle.

'Climbing!' howled Rick. 'You have to be joking! You have to be at least six foot to do that.'

'Shut up, Rick, I can go climbing if I like, and you don't have to be six foot. *Children* go climbing. Theyv'e got boots there from size nine *baby* size upwards, so they must do.'

'Yes, but at *Morgan Castle*!'

I think Rick saw Morgan Castle as a place only for macho boys, and not for girls at all, let alone under-sized freaks like his sister.

'I'll show you,' I said. 'Anyway, I'm not going up the north face of the Eiger.'

'I still think you ought to be six foot,' said Rick, 'even for a small Welsh mountain.'

I was getting really fed up with Rick, in spite of my new mature woman image, and found myself shouting and slapping just as I used to do when I was Baby Face Rosie. Mum got quite exasperated with us over the next few days until she realized it was *Rick* riling *me* and she had a long talk with him one evening. I don't suppose it made him care about his sister any more, but he did stop trying to get my back up.

'He's beginning his adolescence as well, Ros,' she said, one evening when I'd chosen a rather over-ambitious recipe for supper and she'd had to come and help.

'What do you mean, as well?' I demanded. 'I've practically grown out of it.'

'Yes,' she said, 'you have. Most unusually. Except where you and Rick are concerned, that is. Have a bit of patience, love. He's had you for a dominating influence for years, now he wants to do a bit of domi-nating. If we don't battle against him too much he might find there's nothing to fight for and will settle down. It's tedious while it lasts, I know. You went through it as well.'

'Me?' I said, thinking of school where I never had a chance of dominating anyone even if I wanted to.

'Oh, yes. You've always told the boys what to do. And me, sometimes!'

'Well . . . ' I said sheepishly. 'I mean, there they were at school, all thinking I was dear little Rosie . . . '

'Better now?' she inquired.

'I don't think so, but I can cope with it.'

That was what I thought, quite sincerely, folks.

'What an amazing amount of things,' said Marie, scru-tinizing her list of things to take to Morgan Castle. 'I haven't owned any socks for a thousand years. Not since the last Morgan Castle, anyway.'

'Haven't you still got them?' I said. 'I've got mine.' Lovely warm, fluffy-inside, red socks, especially made for wearing inside climbing boots. I didn't go climbing last time, and they were a bit redundant because I didn't go walking either, and there's no point wearing woolly socks in a canoe which you're going to fall our of sometime in the next half hour.

'Lost them,' said Marie. 'Lost and gone for ever. Or more probably obsessively tidied up by my mother. I've got her trained now – she is not, under any circumstances, allowed in my room except on the rare occasions when I've cleared it up myself and can't be bothered to do my own hoovering. Which is about once every two months. But that's fairly recently. When we last went to Morgan Castle she was still chucking out anything I didn't actually put a label on saying "please keep".'

'Honestly?' I was fascinated. Perhaps there was something to be said for being a downtrodden teenager who had to pull her weight at home.

'Doesn't yours?'

'Heavens, no,' I said. 'Has she chucked out your sleeping bag as well, because if she has we've got three.'

'I borrowed one,' she answered. 'This time I'm borrowing Mark's. The same one I had at Easter.'

'Come round tonight and we'll get everything together,' I suggested.

'Sorry, I'm going out.'

With Mark, of course. Silly of me.

It was all so different now. When Marie was going out with Les and Kevin, and before when she had one boyfriend at a time, she still had time for her friends. But Mark was really serious. There was never an evening now when I could go round, casually, and find her there to talk to. Perhaps I still could, but I didn't want to meet Mark again. Not ever.

Still, I thought, cheering up, there'd be a whole week at Morgan Castle when I'd have a friend again. Not only would Mark not be there, but she wouldn't be eyeing up the talent as usual. I could even put up with her telephoning him every evening. And you never knew — there might be some gorgeous hunk who would fall instantly in love with me!

Chapter 9

'This is a good start,' said Aileen, climbing on to the coach with her hair streaming with water.

'I bet it'll be like this all the time,' said Marie, looking out of the coach windows at the pouring rain. 'I'm very, very glad we won't be under canvas. I've had enough of leaky tents.'

'Let's hope we don't have leaky cabins,' I said. 'Do they have central heating?'

'You have to be joking,' said Aileen. 'We're supposed to be hardened, not coddled. Can I change my mind? I've decided I don't want to go after all.'

'What are you doing, Aileen?' I asked. 'If it's canoeing it won't make a lot of difference.'

'True,' she said. 'I did seem to spend more of my time in the water than on top of it last time. Honestly why do we not only volunteer, but *pay*, to be tortured?'

The boys in the group went to the back of the bus and began shouting rude jokes and singing dirty songs before we'd even driven out of the school yard.

Marie raised her eyebrows. 'You can see why people like Mark leave to go to college, can't you?' she said.

I only grunted. If I was going to get Mark, Mark, Mark all the way there, all the time there, and all the way back, I might as well not bother, I thought. And if the talent that I thought I was going to eye up was anything like that lot, then I wasn't going to get very far.

'I thought we were getting sixth formers,' I said to Marie who was settling down in our seat near the front of the bus. 'Where do this lot come from?'

'They're all working terribly solemnly for their exams,' said Marie. 'These are the pre-O level lot. Except for one or two drop-outs I wouldn't touch with a barge-pole anyway.'

'You're not supposed to,' I said. Then, 'I don't know,' seeing a tall, very blond boy just get on the coach. He gazed towards the back, the way people do, searching for a spare seat. He was by himself, and carried a proper rucksack instead of cases and rolls of sleeping bag like the rest of us.

'Dump it there,' said the driver.

'Sorry?'

His voice was marvellous, too. Deep and tingly and

107

expressive. All in that one word.

'Your luggage. Dump it there. We'll put it in the boot later. When the rain stops. Plenty of room.'

'Thanks very much,' said the blond boy. He let the strap slide off his shoulders. Those shoulders! Even under a plaid shirt and a soaking anorak you could see he had muscles on him like – well, not Mr Universe, I find them a bit repulsive myself – but like athletes, you know, runners of marathons. And his tan . . .

'Who is he?' I breathed to Marie.

She turned astonished eyes to me. 'Angus Markham of course.'

'Of course,' I said sarcastically. 'Why haven't I ever seen him or heard of him before?'

'You haven't?' said Marie. 'You must go about with your eyes shut, then. On the other hand . . . he does play rugby, which you refuse to watch, and he does spend most of his time working in the library, which you don't.'

My favourite sport from now on, I knew, was going to be rugby, and I was going to spend all my spare moments in the library, working on all the things I couldn't do.

'Upper sixth, of course?' I hazarded.

'What's wrong with you, Ros?' said Marie, almost crossly. 'He's been everybody's heart-throb for years, and he's been going out with Deborah Street since O levels.'

'Oh, well,' I said. Trust me to pick the ones who aren't available. Still, there was no harm in looking, I told myself, and he really was something to look at.

'What's he doing here, with this mob?' I demanded.

'Hopefully to keep them in order,' said Marie acidly, as the first wave of sweet papers came hurtling down the aisle. 'You'd think they'd stick to one age group. If I'd known about this lot, I wouldn't have come.'

'Too late,' I said as the bus ground into gear and began to move slowly out of the yard into the street. Wipers swept rivulets of water away from the driver's face and steam rapidly obscured the rest of the windows.

Marie sighed and sank back in her seat. 'I don't mind betting it's like this *all* the way and all the time there and begins to brighten up and get really hot the second we get into this coach to come home.'

Aileen leaned over the back of my seat. 'Did you see who came in just then?'

'We did,' drawled Marie.

'He's bust up with her. With Deb, I mean.'

My arms began to tingle. Was there hope yet?

'I *really* fancy him,' said Aileen dreamily.

No. Definitely no hope. Not with Aileen as a rival. With her sleek, beautifully cut auburn hair and her slim legs and fashionable clothes. I looked down at my jeans. You can't look fashionable in jeans when your legs are short. It just is not possible. Nor yet in any other kind of fashionable trousers. The only things which might look a bit like anyone else would be the corduroys which I'd brought for climbing in. They said wear woollen or cotton things, not jeans, because if jeans get wet they apparently cling to you and make you freeze, whereas the other sort are supposed to

109

insulate your legs even when they're soaked. Even so, I'd probably look about ten. You can hardly wear high heels to climb a mountain. Depression was setting in already.

No, the new woman Ros couldn't behave like this! Positive thinking, girl, I told myself severely. At least Dawn wasn't here. There would be absolutely *no* hope then. She just had to fix her sleepy eyes on blokes and they fell like ninepins.

He was sitting somewhere behind us, between us girls and the mob at the back. And it did look as if he was either there officially to keep them behaving moderately well, or had taken it upon himself to do it in the absence of whoever was supposed to be on the coach with us. It seemed a bit strange until we stopped, a few miles up the road, and a very bedraggled PE teacher, Mr Burton, climbed on with his cases.

'I'll put them in later,' grinned the driver, 'when the weather clears up.'

'If it clears up!' returned Mr Burton. He gave us all a smile and a word as he dripped his way down the aisle of the coach, quite different from his normal workaday bad temper and bawling voice. Perhaps, I thought dreamily, watching him slide into the seat next to Angus, perhaps if sporting types were like this in their off-duty hours I could grow to enjoy team games, and hefty men running incomprehensibly on a muddy field.

Then I came down to earth. He wouldn't notice me. Nobody of that sort ever did notice me. There would be no point thinking and hoping. I could only adore from afar, like any first former. One day, perhaps, I would look old and sophisticated instead of small and a bit silly, and people like Angus Markham would notice and be riveted by me.

'What are we doing first?' said Aileen, leaning over the backs of our seats again. 'I lost my programme.'

'Typical,' said Marie. 'Hang on. I think mine's in my bag – no it isn't, it's in my case. In the belly of the bus.'

'I've got mine, you morons,' I said. 'Canoeing, first day,' I read. 'Oh, it's all right, Aileen. Something easy. Shooting rapids.'

She snatched it from me to read what it really said. I knew what I was doing off by heart. Mountain walking first. The rock climbing bit came later, when we were toughened up, I supposed. The last day was abseiling, which we all did.

'Abseiling? What's that when it's at home?' said Aileen. 'I don't remember that from last time.'

'It's all changed since then,' said Marie solemnly. 'Cold showers . . .'

'Diving into the sea from a cliff-top before breakfast,' I continued.

'You do get a choice,' finished Marie, dead-pan.

'But what's this abseiling,' said Aileen, ignoring us.

'It's where you jump off a cliff,' I said.

'Stop the bus, I want to get off,' said Aileen.

'Honestly,' I said. 'Only you've got a rope round you, and you walk backwards off the cliff . . .'

'*Backwards*!'

' . . . and walk down at ninety degrees to the cliff face . . .'

'I feel sick!'

'It's all right,' I assured her. 'It's fun.'

'Sounds it,' said Aileen. 'But I think I'm going to break an ankle before then.'

'In a canoe?' said Marie. 'Hey, look, the sun is shining. What more do you want?'

The mob at the back started cheering. Not because of the sun. They were probably so engrossed in their dirty stories that they hadn't even noticed. But it came at the right moment. We all felt as if it was going to be a great week.

The flat Midlands gave way to rising land, and mountains were already appearing on the horizon. Pretty villages, each one, it seemed, with a spire in the middle, snuggled against the slopes. The sun was hot through the coach windows, and we took off our big sweaters and slung them on to the racks.

'I thought Wales was all coal mines,' said Aileen, looking out at these idyllic scenes.

'This bit isn't,' said Marie. 'The coal mines are South Wales, aren't they? We're going north. Snowdonia.'

I listened and dreamed. Dreamed of climbing Snowdon, leading our party out of a difficult situation where a storm had blown up totally unexpectedly. Deftly I bound up an injured foot, told two of the best orienteers to go down for help while I stayed heroically on the icy slopes with the assault team. The mountain rescue arrived, and I led the rest of the party to the top. Naturally I was the first to reach the summit, and came back down again to see the patient in hospital. I was, of course, warmly congratulated for my presence of mind, knowledge, skill . . .

' . . . do you think, Ros?'

'What?' I said, struggling out of my dreams of glory.

'She hasn't been listening,' said Marie with exasperation. 'Come on, Ros stop dreaming of Angus Markham and tell us what you think.'

And I hadn't even been dreaming of him! There wasn't much hope, I thought, if I couldn't even catch the bloke I fancied in my own day-dream!

And then there was little time for day-dreams, as we drove up to Morgan Castle, a collection, as Marie had said, of wooden huts. Actually, it wasn't as bad as it sounds. The castle itself was a ruin, but the chalets clustered about it were cedarwood, not at all draughty. In fact, when you come back all flushed with health from a strenuous day, it seems a bit too warm inside.

However, that was later. We all, even as staid lower sixth, rushed off the coach and charged over to the office where we'd find out which chalet we'd be in for the week. Another coach drew up as we'd got ourselves all sorted out and disgorged another load of people. Then it was supper, and bed in our youth-hostel-like bunk beds where the eight of us talked until far too late into the night.

The weather couldn't have been more perfect. I joined the group of people who were mountaineering, and we all complained about having to take our big sweaters, and laughed at the sight of our feet in several pairs of socks and mountain boots.

'They must be the smallest climbing boots in existence!' said a girl from the other school, looking down at my feet with incredulity.

'Size four aren't that small,' I said with as much dignity as I could muster, but my heart sank. Here we were again. Little old Ros, the baby of the party. But she was quite nice, really, and attached herself to me, gabbling cheerily as we made a start on the footpath which led to the mountain.

Just you wait, I thought grimly to myself, I haven't done ballet for years for nothing. My muscles will be up to this where yours won't.

But I was wrong. I discovered that climbing muscles were not at all the same as dancing muscles. And my legs, though they could do pirouettes, were shorter than everyone else's. Inevitably, I found myself lagging behind.

The sun burned down on my head, and the pack, containing sweater and my packed lunch, dragged on my back. I saw other packs going in front of me, further and further away.

'Come on, Ros,' called the friendly girl, whose name was Delia.

I stopped, out of breath, and pretended to look back at the way we had come. The mountain dipped below me, the chalets of Morgan Castle very small in the distance. The backs of my legs ached, and I was sure a blister was coming on my heel, in spite of the socks.

Rick and Den were right, I thought miserably. I should never have come.

No, Ros, you can't give up now. Show them what you're made of.

I turned back to the path, and saw the rest still climbing steadily, way ahead of me. I made a terrific effort, and punished my legs to catch up with them.

Doggedly, my legs on fire, I climbed, looking down at the path so that I shouldn't be put off by the widening gap, and then suddenly came upon them, sitting comfortably on slabs of Welsh rock, eating chocolate.

Our leader, Mr Burton, grinned at me as I staggered to a halt and sat down with them. 'Keeping up all right, Ros?' he said.

You know damned well I'm not, I said to myself miserably, but I nodded, too out of breath to speak.

'All right. Shall we go on?'

They all groaned, me most of all, because I could really have done with a good rest there. My legs were trembling. I didn't know whether I'd make it.

'Come on, Rosie,' said Delia.

'Want a haul up, Titch?' said one of the boys. One of the fourth year boys. I could have died with shame and humiliation.

'No, thanks,' I said frostily. 'I can manage for myself.'

'She's a big girl now,' said another boy, 'stopped wearing nappies a week ago.'

I tried to laugh, to join in the joke against me. It was the only defence. I refused to behave like a small child again. I'd had enough of that with Mark.

It was the best thing to do. They laughed at me, but it didn't stop them mocking as I struggled behind the team again. Thank goodness the fabulous Angus Markham wasn't there. If I was going to put on any kind of sparkling show for him during the evening, when I could wear my high heels, I didn't want him prejudiced by my non-performance during the day.

To be honest I didn't even see who was on my team, except for Delia and Mr Burton. I was too busy grimly forcing my shorter steps to keep up with everyone else. And trying to catch my breath when they stopped for their rests and waited for me.

'That's where we're going to do rock climbing,' said Mr Burton, waving his arm over to a fearsome looking sheer face over to our right.

'Oh, no!' groaned Delia. 'I've decided I haven't got a head for heights after all.'

'You're not serious—' said the boy who had called me Titch.

'Never been so serious in my life,' said Mr Burton. 'But don't worry. I wouldn't let any of you amateurs on the high pitches. We'll just learn a bit of technique on the lower slopes.'

'Pitches? What pitches, sir?'

'Football pitch, sir?'

'Honestly,' breathed Delia in my ear, 'they're so *young*!'

My grin back at her was out of all proportion, How marvellous it was, at least, to feel old, one of the more responsible members of the team.

'I don't fancy climbing with that lot,' I said. I couldn't trust them with a belay.'

'A what?' said Delia.

'Haven't you done any climbing before?' I asked.

'None,' she said. 'And I don't know why I said I would now, except that I like hill walking and the rock climbing came into it. I think I might suddenly be terribly ill, one of those viruses, you know? I suppose you know all about rock climbing?'

'Not a thing,' I said cheerfully. 'Only what I've seen on TV and read about. Chris Bonnington and all that. It's all very well knowing all the technical terms, but I should think I'll be as bad at that as I am at hill walking.'

'What's it like to be so small?' said Delia.

Thump. Back again. I didn't think I could bear it.

And we weren't to go rock climbing today. We had to finish this awful walk, which wasn't any easier for me downhill than it had been up. I wasn't quite so out of breath, but I still got left behind, and it was getting really embarrassing that they had to keep waiting for me to catch up.

'Come on, Rosie Posie, trot trot trot,' called Mr Burton. Even Mr Burton. I was so miserable, I wanted to go home.

Perhaps it would be better this evening, when we could sit around and talk and play tapes on the cassette player in the common room, or have a go at chess or cards. You didn't have to be a giant to do that.

But the sight of me running along behind seemed to amuse everyone so much that they couldn't leave it alone, especially at supper time. People kept offering to cut up my meat for me, or spoon potato into my mouth. I did laugh and pretend to play along with it, but I was intensely miserable. Mostly because Marie joined in with them, and didn't stick up for me at all. Only Delia said once, 'Oh, shut up, you lot, I'm sick of your infantile jokes.' But it didn't do any good.

And no one put on high heels for the evening. Mind you, we were all so footsore that padding around in socks and jeans seemed the most sensible thing. And Aileen, when she had finished telling our group about how she nearly tipped their canoe over by paddling too fiercely into the water, went off with Marie and the others who were doing the water sports. I did notice – how could I help it – that she sat in an old armchair right next to Angus Markham. I presumed he'd been on the canoeing team. He certainly hadn't been with us.

Perhaps I could change to canoeing. Or did you need long arms for that? I couldn't remember. If things weren't any better tomorrow, I'd certainly ask if I could change over.

Or go home.

I wanted suddenly, desperately, to go home. I don't normally get homesick, and if anyone had asked me last week what it felt like, I wouldn't have been able to tell them. I knew now. It was a dark, heavy feeling at the base of your throat and in your chest. If it rose, you knew, you would either panic or cry. In fact, I felt that if anyone else made any more cracks about my baby face I'd burst into tears.

Someone did. I didn't. Which made me feel a bit better. Still, I began to make silly plans about how I could go home if I really couldn't bear things any longer. There ought to be a bus somewhere. I could get a bus to the nearest big town. Then go home by train. I'd got enough money with me, money to buy a sweat-shirt with the castle printed on it, money to buy souvenirs for the family at home.

I'd give it one more day, that was all.

Chapter 10

I suppose I knew my friendship with Marie was really over now. Not that we would ever be enemies, but after Mark, and now being in a different team, and finally her joining in the jokes when she knew how sensitive I was about my height, we didn't seem to have anything in common any more.

I felt even more gloomy as we plodded our way up the mountain again. Everything seemed to have happened to me all at once. I'd found two boyfriends, lost both of them, and now lost my best friend as well. And then, after deciding I was now going to behave like a mature woman in spite of my size, it was all blown to pieces on this horrible mountain.

I felt dull, panting up and up, the same as yesterday. The rest of them seemed to do it on purpose, waiting for me until I caught up and then rushing off again. I was determined not to ask them to wait for me to have a rest. I wouldn't give them any more reason to laugh at me than they had already.

It didn't, in fact, seem so far to the rocks we were to

climb as it had the day before. I suppose knowing how far it was made it seem shorter. I sat down, glad at last to have an excuse, and let everyone else clamour to have a go first.

There were complaints and moans, of course, when they discovered they weren't going to do amazing feats of daring, standing out like flies on the top of a hundred-foot cliff, though I think I saw a few concealed looks of relief as well. We were only to practise balancing on our fingers and boot toes on slabs of rock right by the grassy plateau on which we stood.

'Come on, Ros, are you having a go?'

'What? No ropes?' I said. 'Sure I won't fall off that bit?'

It was all of five feet high but I wanted to get the jokes in first.

'See how you get on,' said Mr Burton, 'then you can go a bit higher with a leader if you want.'

'Will we have to rescue her, sir, if she yells on the top?' said one of the fourth formers.

'More likely she'll have to rescue you,' said Mr Burton, who had by now had as much as I'd had of this.

I concentrated hard, and found I was really enjoying myself. Ballet gives you a good sense of balance, which I had naturally anyway, and I knew that to stay balanced I mustn't lean backwards at all, which most of them were doing and falling off in wild heaps.

'That's very good,' said Mr Burton, coming up beside me. 'No, don't try to get up with your knees.

You'll find you haven't any strength and you'll lose your balance. Get your foot there if possible.'

The rock was solid, with no crumbling pieces. It had obviously been climbed on a lot and anything that might have fallen had fallen ages ago. My fingers went for tiny knobs, my feet balanced on slim cracks.

Round me there were pants and yells and curses as people with big feet tried to lift their unsupple legs on to projectories which they could balance on.

'Can I try to go higher?' I asked demurely, having done all the little exercises other people were struggling with.

'Sure,' said Mr Burton, 'if you can wait a bit. Have a rest — I've got to deal with this mob for the moment. But Dave Cullen is on his way — I think I saw his yellow anorak about five minutes ago past that buttress. Then if I'm still tied up with this lot he can lead you. There's a moderately difficult pitch I think you could manage very well. It's us lot with big feet who can't do it. There's another one with a chimney as well, if you're interested tomorrow perhaps, that we tend to get stuck in if we're not careful.'

'Who's Dave Cullen?' I asked casually, revelling in this new appreciation of my meagre size.

'Equivalent of Angus Markham,' he said, 'belongs to Paxton.'

Paxton High School was the other lot who had come to Morgan Castle with us, and to whom most of the fourth-year boys in our climbing team belonged. I didn't know whether I wanted to be taught how to climb anything more complicated by some stuck-up upper-sixth former who would probably make more infantile comments about my size. Still, perhaps Mr Burton would be able to let him take over the Paxton lot instead, while he took me higher on the cliff face.

'What worries me,' said Delia, coming to sit down with me as I waited, 'is how you get down. Not that it will probably affect me much. I can't get up yet.'

'But it's easy,' I said, really meaning it.

'Not to me it isn't,' said Delia. 'I don't mind the height, I've discovered, but I really don't know how to stay on one square millimetre of friable rock.'

'Press down with your soles,' I said, 'and don't let your foot bend.'

'You have to be joking,' she said. 'My foot not only bends, it wobbles, and so do my knees. No, I can't see me getting any further than that two foot boulder.'

'At least you won't have to worry about getting down,' I grinned.

We watched the yellow anorak come steadily up the mountain path which we had ascended ourselves only an hour or two before.

'Oh, well,' said Delia, sighing, 'I'd better try, I suppose. Isn't it lunch time yet?'

'Should be,' I said, looking at my watch. 'Shall I suggest it?'

'That's the best idea I've heard today,' said Delia. 'In that case, I'll have one last go and if I can't get any higher than two feet I'll give up.'

I called over to Mr Burton that I thought it was time

122

for lunch, and he gave up struggling with a couple of idiots – the ones, I was glad to see, who had been most rude about me trotting about behind – and declared a break.

I didn't really look at the newcomer. I was busy talking to Delia and trying to show her how to cling on to the smaller holds while looking for something else a bit more solid. I even took her over to the flake where we'd practised some of the more difficult holds and showed her. And my half a term of teaching ballet came in useful as well – not that I was trying to teach her ballet or anything like it, but I did know about balance and how to achieve it.

'If you've had lunch, Ros, we might try that pitch now,' came Mr Burton's voice behind me. I looked across at the rest of the team. Dave Cullen seemed to be working with the fourth years from his own school. I was quite relieved. I didn't want to have to get to know yet another person, not while I was feeling so good about this rock-climbing business.

'Can you tie a bowline?' he asked, throwing the end of an immensely stiff rope at me. 'Sorry, it's a bit new, but at least you'll know it's safe.'

'No,' I said. 'I can do reefs and grannies, and I once managed a sheep-shank, though I can't remember how to now and I never knew what it was for.'

'Probably just as well,' he said, 'because you'd have done it holding the rope in front of you and I want you to do it with the rope round your waist. It looks quite different that way. All right, take the short end in your right hand, over the long bit in your left, underneath, round the long bit and pull back. Now tighten it, and there you are.'

'I'll never be able to do that again,' I said, testing the feel of it round my waist.

'Undo it and try,' he said. 'Not difficult really. It's a non-slipping knot. You don't want your waist squeezed into a five-inch circumference when you fall off, do you?'

'I'm not going to fall off,' I said with certainty.

'Oh, yes, you are,' he said. 'I'm going to ask you to fall – one of the essentials in any dangerous sport. Then you won't be afraid of it and do something daft.'

'Right,' I sighed. 'Is that okay?' I showed him my second attempt at a bowline.

'Well,' he said, 'pull . . . ' And the knot tightened round my waist.

I got it right eventually, and then we started. He went up first, then belayed, that is, fixed himself to an immovable – I hoped – piece of rock, then I went up. It was as easy as that. And if I didn't look down I didn't get scared. It wasn't at all bad. Half-way up he decided I was good enough to try the famous chimney, so we did a traverse (I was getting good at the technical terms as well) and began to squeeze our way into the narrow confines. I heard him gasping and swearing as he tried to force his body up the funnel. The rope snaked up in front of me, then it was my turn.

I braced my back against the rock sides and shuffled with my feet flat against the opposite wall. It was a doddle. I came out at the top saying innocently, 'Haven't you got anything more difficult than this?'

Mr Burton just snarled at me, then grinned and said he'd had enough.

So had I, by this time. For a first day on the rocks I'd really done a tremendous lot. It was great to feel that I'd done things the rest couldn't, and that I'd made a success of it.

Perhaps I wouldn't go home after all! I laughed at myself, at my yesterday self, for thinking I would. I ate supper with a vast appetite and nobody – nobody except one of our own stupid fourth years – said anything about cutting my meat up.

'How'd you get on?' I asked Marie when I had taken the edge off my hunger and was ready to eat the rest a bit more slowly.

'Absolute hell,' she said frankly. 'I've decided that I don't like shooting rapids at all. I'll leave them to people in the movies. It is *not* my scene. Though I quite liked it out at sea yesterday. That's where I'm going tomorrow. And I've fallen in about seventy times and got soaked to the skin and I'm sure I'll get pneumonia before tomorrow anyway, so I'll have to be shipped home by helicopter.'

'*Can* you get shipped . . .' began Aileen incautiously.

'*You* know what I mean,' snarled Marie.

Actually, you could see she missed Mark. After supper she went straight to the students' phone by the office and didn't come back for ages, not until we'd started a sing-song because we'd decided the tapes they'd got there were absolutely useless and we could do a great deal better.

I was suddenly aware that somebody, somebody rather tall, dark and good-looking, was sitting beside me. I turned my head to look, and found he was staring right into my eyes and smiling at me.

Dave Cullen.

He didn't look at all the same in his casual gear as he did in an anorak and thick trousers. His hair, instead of being all over the place in the wind, was carefully combed and neat. The open-necked shirt was white, and the tan on his bare arms was golden.

I took all this in in a fraction of a second, then pulled my head away nervously.

'I'm sorry, I don't know your name,' he said in the gap between two verses.

'Rosalind,' I said. Why Rosalind? I'd always been Ros, or Rosie, except to Miss Libetta.

'I haven't seen you before,' he said.

'I haven't seen *you*,' I said, 'until this afternoon.' I was disappointed. Had my climbing performance been so mediocre that he hadn't noticed?

'This afternoon?' He was plainly puzzled.

'On the rocks. You were helping the fourth-year boys.'

'I didn't know you – wait a minute, weren't you the one who did the chimney with John Burton?'

'That's right,' I said.

'Pretty good,' he said. 'I can't do it. My body won't fold up enough.'

126

'That's the beauty of being short,' I said, and almost kicked myself because here I was already, calling attention to something I didn't want noticed – as if anybody wouldn't notice, eventually.

'Are you?' he said, and I could have hugged him, there and then, even with Marie just back from the phone and coming across the room in her elegant new trousers with the matching casual jacket and high heels. I was painfully aware of my turned up jeans, my less-than-best sweater, even though my own high heels made me feel a lot better even sitting down. Damn you, Marie, I thought to myself, why do you have to out-shine *everybody*, especially me, just when I'm beginning to get to know . . .

He turned away from the vision and looked at me again. He wasn't interested! He truly wasn't interested. He must be the only bloke in the whole wide world who has looked at Marie Johnson and not been dazed. And it wasn't because he felt he had to turn away quickly before anyone noticed how attracted he was. He just *wasn't*.

'I've just phoned home,' said Marie.

'I know,' I said. 'How was Mark?'

I just had to put this in, so that Dave knew she was already going out with someone. I suppose it was a bit mean, but even when Marie is head over heels in love with someone she just can't help looking as if she's interested in any other man she meets. I wondered how Aileen was managing in her bid for Angus, with Marie around.

But I was being uncharitable. She didn't mean it. She

never does. She's just her.

'He wasn't in,' she said. 'I was talking to my parents.'

'Would you trust me climbing with you tomorrow?' said Dave. To me.

Would I? I'd go to the ends of the earth . . .

'Love to,' I said.

'I really don't know how I never noticed you before. Except that I really admired that chimney climb. Where were you? And you haven't done any climbing before? I really do find that hard to believe.'

I was dazzled, completely and utterly. And Dave didn't seem to notice Marie existed. After a while she removed herself and went and sat over the other side of the room, rather disconsolately talking to someone else.

I felt suddenly sorry for her. I hadn't even listened properly when she said Mark wasn't in at her home, and she must have felt really miserable about it. But I couldn't go over to her now. Not now that this wonderful Dave was talking to me. How had I ever thought Angus Markham was attractive? Dave Cullen could knock spots off him.

'Well, for a start,' I said, 'I'm at a different school. I'm from Queen Elizabeth's.'

'Which would explain a great deal,' he said. 'But I don't know why I haven't noticed you here before. I mean . . .'

He didn't say what he meant, so I was able to day-dream what he might have meant. Like 'I mean you stand out so much with your gorgeous curly hair and your huge blue eyes'. Or 'I admired the way you walked up the hill after the rock climbing . . . '

I came down to earth with a bump again. Perhaps it was as well he hadn't said anything after 'I mean . . . ' What he probably *did* mean was that he ought to have noticed old shorty, titch, dwarf – any of the names I've been called in my time.

He was still looking at me.

'I mean,' he went on slowly, 'those eyes of yours. Enough to knock a bloke sideways.'

Eyes. I'd dreamed eyes. Not *size*. No, I couldn't have mistaken what he said.

'Tell me,' he said, 'you seem very knowledgeable about climbing. And yet you say you haven't done any before. Got brothers who do?'

'I'm actually interested in it, believe it or not,' I said. 'I watch everything they do on TV – which isn't very much, and not nearly enough for me. Did you see that marvellous climb where they did the Old Man of Hoy? Years ago.'

And Mum had had to video it for me, because I was at orchestra. Orchestra! How many years ago did I go there?

'It's my ambition,' he said, 'to go to Everest. I don't care if I don't climb it, I just want to go there, to see the base camp . . . '

' . . . and be in those mountains. The roof of the world,' I said. 'Did you know you can actually go there on a holiday – a sort of package tour – walking through the foothills to base camp? I read about it in a travel article in one of the Sunday papers. You have to

129

take about three weeks, because of the altitude . . . '

We went on talking all evening, through the songs and the tapes when everybody got fed up with singing, through the games of Monopoly and brag. And then it was tea and biscuits, and time to go off to our chalets.

Marie joined me as we yawned out into the darkness. I was quite glad of her company by now because I thought Dave might have offered to walk with me. But he didn't. He just said, 'See you tomorrow, then,' in a coolly friendly way, waved his hand and went off to round up his gang of fourth-years.

'So that's Dave Cullen,' she said.

'Who's Dave Cullen?'

'Who you've been talking to, you fool,' she said.

'No, I know that, you burk. What I mean is, you said, "So that's Dave Cullen" as if he was a film star or something.'

'Oh, no. Just the bloke all the girls are crazy about, that's all.'

'Like Angus Markham,' I said.

'Something like that,' she said.

She was silent as we crossed the turf to Number Five. Then, at the door, 'Is he nice?' as if she wanted to apologize for Mark again.

'Very,' I said. Then I relented. 'Didn't you get through to Mark, then?'

'He hadn't been near our house, and I said I'd phone at seven. And he didn't even turn up while I was talking to Mum and Dad. That's why I was so long. I kept on putting in ten pences in case he did arrive.'

'Poor Marie,' I said. 'I bet you're really fed up. But

there's bound to be a good reason. He probably missed the bus.'

'How dare he miss the bus when I'm phoning him?' said Marie. 'He should have got to the stop early enough. Men!'

'Going to try phoning again now?' I said.

'No,' said Marie. 'First I haven't any money left, and second he can bloody well worry about me for a change, so there.'

I laughed. 'If it wasn't Mark, I'd believe you.'

She blushed. 'Well – you know – in fact what I shall probably do is cry all night, but I'm not going to phone again.'

'Poor Mark,' I said.

There were running footsteps which came in our direction.

'Are either of you Marie Johnson?' panted a girl from Paxton.

'I am,' said Marie.

'There's a telephone call for you, in the office.'

'Mark,' I said.

'You're not supposed to phone the office except in an emergency, even if the student phone is engaged,' said the girl from Paxton. 'I suppose it's your parents.'

'Nosy,' I said. 'Anyway, this is an emergency, isn't it Marie?'

But she had already gone.

Chapter 11

We were so tired, that second night, that I don't think anyone talked for more than about five minutes after the lights were out. I felt Marie moving in the top bunk above me, than there was stillness and silence.

But though I was absolutely shattered, I couldn't sleep. The image of a dark, good-looking bloke kept passing in front of my eyes, and I went over and over all the nice things he had said to me. And all the things he hadn't said, which was even sweeter. It generally wasn't long before some idiot said something about my size. He hadn't. He'd treated me like a normal human being.

Honestly, I chided myself, you sound as if you think you were some sort of freak. You're getting really silly about this height business. Dammit, some people actually *want* to be small!

He said he noticed my eyes . . .

I drifted into dreams.

Dreams are all very well. You can make things happen the way you want them. But when we were all outside, waiting for Mr Burton to arrive, I was in a state of real panic. Suppose he didn't recognize me?

Suppose he'd got a girlfriend somewhere at home, whom he rang every evening like Marie rang Mark? That was obviously why he'd rushed off supposedly getting the fourth years to their chalets.

I tried to hide behind the crowd of people, It wasn't that difficult. When Mr Burton came up I tagged along at the back – my normal place, anyway, I thought bitterly – and once again I had to keep up with them. Although, when we were on the mountain path I found my muscles were responding a lot better, everyone else's were too, so they still went on ahead, waiting for me to catch up every so often.

And Dave Cullen wasn't there.

After all that I was so disappointed that I felt as if there was a great leaden weight in my throat. Who cared if I could climb narrow chimneys? Who cared if I could get up flakes of rock with tiny holds on them? Those with bigger feet and stronger hands would be able to get up the longer climbs better than I would. My initial advantage would soon be cancelled out.

I tramped along glumly, looking sideways at the view and wishing I was happy enough to appreciate it. I heard the tramp of someone's feet coming up behind me, steadily, but I wasn't even interested enough to turn round.

'I'm glad you waited, Rosalind,' said the voice which I knew I would recognize anywhere in the world.

'I didn't,' I said. Might as well be honest, right from the start. 'I couldn't keep up.'

He stood, feet apart on the narrow track, grinning at me. 'Better that way,' he said. 'You don't want to use up all your energy before you get there. I need a rest. Do you mind sitting down for a moment or two?'

Me? Mind having a rest? I was *desperate* for a rest. And I could sit half-way up a mountain with Dave Cullen any time you asked me to.

'Chocolate? I did have breakfast, but those boys wear me out. I feel I need sustenance.'

He unfolded the silver paper, broke off two squares and handed them to me.

'Thanks,' I said. 'Do you have to look after them?'

'Well, I suppose not officially, but I've been here before and know the place, and they're a bit of a handful for one member of staff to cope with, aren't they?'

'True,' I agreed. 'We've got a sixth former who seems to do the same thing.'

'Angus? Nice bloke. We usually climb together.'

Oh dear. Now he was going to find out how pitifully inadequate I was. That is, if he'd remembered he was going to climb with me today anyway. Probably not. He'd be going with Mr Burton, showing the rest of us what could be done, and I'd be left on the short, easy climbs, with everyone else.

'Shall we move on?'

The others were completely out of sight. I didn't care. I was with Dave Cullen, the nicest boy I'd ever met in my life. I didn't care if he was being kind, asking if *he* could have a rest when it was obvious he could see it was *I* who needed one. There was something to be said for tactful kindness. I decided that perhaps my mother's fierce honesty could have its disadvantages.

'Sorry we're late but Rosalind waited for me and I needed a bit of a rest on the way,' he called to Mr Burton as we neared the mob by the rock face.

'I know how you feel,' said Mr Burton, coming over to us. 'Of course, we've had a day's advantage over you. If you must take people with broken legs to hospital . . . '

'Sorry, John,' he grinned. 'Unavoidable. Is it all right if I take Rosalind up some of the moderately difficult climbs?'

He *did* mean it!

'Good idea. Leave the rest of them to me. Okay by you, Ros?'

'Sure,' I said, feeling my smile stretch to my cheekbones.

Now all I had to do, I thought, was to forget how to do that darned bowline and he'd revise his opinion of me completely. I don't know how I *did* remember how to do it, but I did, and at a comfortable distance from my waist as well, not tight, but not so loose that it would lift over my head at the first sign of strain.

'Do you want to do the first pitch?' said Dave casually.

'I don't think – I mean – could—'

'I don't see why not. I'll tell you how to belay, then I'll take over and lead from there.'

'You'll have to. I wouldn't know what to do.'

'Yes, you do. You watched John Burton yesterday. Go up as far as you think the rope will take you, then belay to a nice solid piece of rock.'

He showed me what to do, and we had a practice

down on the grassy base, pretending it was a convenient shelf to stand on while pulling in the rope from above. It seemed very complicated, with karabiner snap-links and slings and the right kinds of knots, but he seemed to think I'd got it all right and before I had time to protest I found myself at the bottom of the long, though not difficult, climb called Sailor's Drop.

At least, it seemed long to me. I've never known time go by so slowly as it did on that first pitch. And yet, if I'd fallen off it would have been only a few feet, and I'd have dropped quite easily on to the grass below. I suppose it was the thought that I'd got to do something which, higher up, could save someone's life, and I didn't know whether I'd be able to do it properly.

'Well done,' came Dave's voice from below as I climbed steadily to the little ledge which he'd pointed out to me. There had been a better-looking ledge, I thought, a little further up, but he said there wasn't a very good place to belay from there. I found the projecting piece of rock. Just right, I thought professionally, for an anchorage. I stood on the ledge, did all the things I'd been told, and shouted 'Okay!'

I took up the slack in the rope as he climbed, making sure it was just pulled up enough so that it didn't interfere with his climbing, feeling the rope across the back of my anorak, and then—

I braced myself as the strain cut into my shoulder when he slipped momentarily and I had his full weight on me.

But the belay held, and the rope held, and I held on tight. I closed my eyes as his feet scrabbled and little chunks of rock rattled down the face.

Mr Burton had made me slip, just like that, yesterday. So that I should feel perfectly safe even as I'd swung, ridiculously, trying to grab hold of something solid as I wobbled round like a crazed pendulum. But was Dave safe? I forgot the fact that he was only two feet from the ground.

There is nothing like falling off to make you feel safe. And there is nothing like someone else falling off to make you feel you might, after all, know roughly what you're doing.

And then I found I didn't have any fear of the height at all. Dave came up to me, stopped briefly on the ledge to say, 'Well done,' and then went on upwards. I paid out the rope as I had pulled it in before. I felt as if I was standing on a ledge on top of the world, and it felt marvellous!

And then I found I was looking with a professional eye on the lumps and projections, measuring the distances between this foothold and that handhold so that when it was my turn to climb up I knew exactly where I meant to go.

'You're going to make a very good climber,' said Dave when I reached him on his ledge. 'But I think it would be as well if I kept on leading, don't you?'

'I never thought otherwise,' I said. It was *very* narrow on this ledge, and I was very conscious of him pressing against me. 'See you at the top.'

He sounded amused. 'There's a few more pitches till we get to the top,' he said. 'Are you okay? Don't want to go down?'

I looked down. It wasn't a good idea. I didn't mind about the distance, but the thought of searching for all those little cracks with my toenails made my stomach heave.

'How do you . . . ?' I began, then thought this wasn't the best of questions since I hadn't even got up there yet.

'Get down? We'll have a bit of fun, shall we? Do some abseiling before the rest of them. Not officially on the programme till tomorrow, but it's much easier than scrambling down the back.'

'Scrambling down the *what*?'

'Behind this cliff is a nice, grass-covered slope. When you get to the top all you do is walk sedately down the other side.'

'Or scramble,' I quoted. 'But that's cheating!'

'So it is,' he agreed. 'That's why we're going to abseil.'

'Wonderful,' I said uncertainly.

'So are you,' he said, and before I realized what was happening he kissed me, right on the lips, half-way up this cliff face as we hung like two spiders from heavy-duty web-silk. I was so stunned, thrilled, enchanted, that I nearly fell off, and if his arm hadn't been firmly round me I probably would have.

There was a faint derisive cheer from below.

'Hell,' he said. 'It never occurred to me that they'd be watching. Stupid of me. I suppose we are a bit exposed up here . . . '

'I don't care,' I said. I'd shout it from the mountain

tops, and not care if the whole of Wales heard me.

'Okay,' and he laughed, his teeth startlingly white in the tan of his face. 'We'll give them another thrill on the next stop. I'm going now. Hold tight.'

And with that he swung away, his long legs scratching on the rock surface, the kick of his boot toes and the faint clink of the karabiners the only sounds in our tiny exposed world.

'I don't know that it's very safe, doing this, half-way up a cliff face,' I said unsteadily when I got up to the next ledge and got my promised kiss. 'You're making my knees shake.'

'Want a rest?' he said. 'We've got an overhang next. Actually, I shouldn't have brought you up this way — it's supposed to be a difficult standard, but I thought you were coping so well . . .'

'I don't mind,' I said. 'It's not the climbing.'

'Sorry. Better save that for later. I don't want to make your knees shake: that overhang will do it without me helping.' And then, as he fumbled with the packet of chocolate to ease out the last two squares, 'Do you mind?'

'Mind what? The overhang?'

'No. Me kissing you. Because I just couldn't help it. You're so gorgeous.'

'I don't mind,' I whispered. 'I don't mind at all.' In fact, kiss me as much as you like, I thought, suddenly feeling bleak, because at the end of this holiday we'll go back to our respective schools and won't ever see each other again.

I told myself to numb my mind. To concentrate on the climb. Not to think about the future. It doesn't matter. Now is all that matters.

'Can you manage?'

I looked at the overhang. It didn't look too awful. Not even very overhung, really.

'I'll watch what you do,' I said.

'After that, it's just a scramble to the top,' he said. 'We could have our lunch there before coming down, couldn't we?'

'But I've left mine at the bottom,' I said.

'I thought of that,' said Dave. 'What do you think I carry in this pack? It's not just ice-picks and chocolate and yesterday's *Times*, you know!'

I giggled. It hadn't occurred to me to wonder what he was carrying. I only remember thinking it must make life even more difficult with that to balance on your back. I suppose I might have thought he was carrying it for practice – for the Himalayas or something.

'Will you have enough for me as well?' I asked.

'I always bring double, just in case,' he assured me solemnly.

I wasn't sure whether I liked that. In case what? In case he should manage to entice some unsuspecting female to the top of a mountain with him?

'No, truly,' he said, 'it's in case I go too far, or have an accident or something and need to survive for two days before the rescue party arrives. It's never stupid to be over-prepared on a mountain.'

'Will you get on with that overhang?' I said,

ashamed of thinking what I'd been thinking. 'The more I look at it the more nervous I get. I wish you hadn't told me what it was. It was all right when it just looked like a jutting out bit.'

'That's all it is,' said Dave cheerfully. 'See you at the top.'

I watched, carefully, and it didn't seem too bad. But then he had his long body to help him. I wasn't sure whether I was going to be able to curve myself over like he had. Oh, well, I thought philosophically, you only live once. And anyway, I was quite safely roped on.

It was absolute hell.

I don't think I've ever been so frightened in my life. This great shelf came looming out at me, and I seemed to be underneath it, then upside down, then dangling in an undignified way with one foot over the top of the shelf and the other hanging in space. I don't know where my hands were: clinging on by their fingernails I should think, judging by the state of them when I got to the top.

'That,' I said panting, 'was *horrible*.'

'I'm not surprised,' he said. 'You went the wrong way. There was an easier bit.'

'Oh. Sorry. Ros messes it up again.'

'No, you didn't. You were marvellous. I couldn't have done that on my first day climbing.'

'Second,' I corrected.

'Or my twentieth,' he said.

'But you told me what to do.'

'Even if anyone had told me what to do,' he said. 'You certainly deserve your lunch.'

'Are we at the top?' I said, surprised. It didn't look like top to me.

'A last scramble. Just a scramble. And then we're there.'

I honestly didn't know whether I had the strength, but somehow I made it. If I hadn't just done that terrible overhang I'd probably have found it as easy as climbing on to a park bench, but I had been thoroughly shaken by Dave, as well as the climb.

We sat on the short grass, biting wind shaving our ears, and opened the sandwiches. They were the ordinary thick white bread and Spam ones, provided by the centre, but I've never tasted anything so marvellous in all my life. He'd even brought a couple of cans of Lilt with him. Nectar.

'How you managed to carry this lot up, especially on that last bit . . . ' I said.

'Practice,' he said. 'I'll give you a pack to carry on the last day.'

'That's abseiling,' I reminded him.

'*They're* going to be abseiling,' he corrected. '*We* are going climbing. Heavens, I can't stop just when I've found a decent partner.'

'You really think I'll be all right?' I said, glowing.

'You know you're all right, Rosalind,' he said. He looked at me seriously for a moment. 'In fact, I don't really know how . . . You're so different, so much older than any other girl I've ever met. I don't mean,' he said hastily, 'old, but more – *mature* – if you know what I mean.'

I didn't, but I didn't care. He thought I was the new

mature Rosalind. I would never again be Baby Face.

We practised a new, mature kiss. It didn't matter if my legs went wobbly now.

'Want to abseil down?'

'I don't think I ever want to reach the bottom again,' I said dreamily. 'I'd really like to stay up here for ever.'

'There's tomorrow,' he said.

'And the next day,' I said. I stopped myself. I mustn't expect this to last beyond this holiday.

'I looked up your address in the office this morning,' he said. 'I hope you don't mind. We only live about half a mile apart. Can I go on seeing you when we get back? You haven't got a steady boyfriend, have you?'

'No,' I said. 'I haven't got a steady boyfriend.'

'So will you be my partner?' he said softly. 'When we get home as well?'

I gave him my answer. It was all very satisfactory.

Pam Lyons
Danny's Girl £1.25

For sixteen-year-old Wendy, life was pretty straightforward. She enjoyed her tomboy existence with her parents and brother Mike on their farm in Norfolk. Then, late one sunny September afternoon, Danny wandered into her life and suddenly Wendy's happy and uncomplicated world is turned upside-down. Unsure of how she should behave or what is expected of her, she allows herself to be carried along in Danny's wake, and when he finds himself in trouble at his exclusive boarding school she is his only ally. Eventually, Wendy's fierce loyalty to the boy she loves leads them both deeper and deeper into trouble . . .

David S. Williams
Forgive and Forget £1.25

Claire's life was in turmoil when her family moved to Wales. It meant leaving Simon, the guy who meant so much to her, and she was determined *never* to like her new home. But the rugged beauty of the countryside and the compelling friendliness of the people soothed away her resentment. And then she met Gareth, a dark-eyed Welsh boy who captivated her with his infectious grin . . .

These books are available at your local bookshop or newsagent, or can be ordered direct from the publisher. Indicate the number of copies required and fill in the form below
....

Name ———————————————————————————
(Block letters please)

Address ———————————————————————————

———————————————————————————————

Send to CS Department, Pan Books Ltd,
PO Box 40, Basingstoke, Hants
Please enclose remittance to the value of the cover price plus:
35p for the first book plus 15p per copy for each additional book ordered to a maximum charge of £1.25 to cover postage and packing
Applicable only in the UK

While every effort is made to keep prices low, it is sometimes necessary to increase prices at short notice. Pan Books reserve the right to show on covers and charge new retail prices which may differ from those advertised in the text or elsewhere